The Dom's Submission series

His Sub

Book 1

Ellis O. Day

I love to hear from readers so email me at
authorellisoday@gmail.com

https://www.EllisODay.com

Facebook
https://www.facebook.com/EllisODayRomanceAuthor/

Closed FB Group (sneak peeks, sample chapters, and other bonuses)
https://www.facebook.com/groups/153238782143373

Twitter
https://twitter.com/ellis_o_day

Pinterest
www.pinterest.com\AuthorEllisODay

Ellis O. Day

(AVAILABLE IN PAPERBACK AND EBOOK)

PART ONE – HIS SUB

CHAPTER 1: Terry

Terry wandered through the crowd of well-dressed women and men at La Petite Mort Club. It was the same scene every time Ethan, his friend and owner of the Club, threw one of these events. The members mingled with the newbies, hoping to snag something different or someone interesting.

Ethan strolled casually toward him, a ready smile on his face as he greeted his guests. "Terry, about time you made it down here."

"Like you can talk." His friend spent most of the time in the back office, watching the Club on monitors.

"I've been mingling for over an hour."

"It's your business not mine." He leaned against the balustrade, peering down on the crowd.

"True, but you could sell your practice and buy me out."

"And run this place?" He laughed. "No, thank you." He tossed back his scotch. "I spend enough time here as it is." He used to practically live here except when he was at the office or in court, but lately he'd been staying home more.

"Good turn out tonight." Ethan waved at a waitress and a moment later they each had another drink.

"Yeah, but I don't see one interesting person in this crop of wannabe members."

"And you can tell if someone is interesting just by looking at them?"

"I can tell not one of them has an original thought. Look at them. They're all in red." The Club was awash in a sea of red dresses—short, long, dark, light but always red.

"It is a Valentine's Day party."

"I know but you'd think one woman"—he held up his finger—"one would consider that everyone else would be in red and wear a different color."

"There are some pinks out there."

"Same thing, just lighter."

Ethan grabbed his phone from his pocket and looked at the text, frowning.

"Problem?" The Club was usually a safe place but on open night events, when Ethan allowed non-members access in order to recruit new members, the place could get dangerous.

"A little skirmish over a woman." Ethan grinned, his blue eyes sparkling as a couple of young guys hurried past them, almost tripping in their haste to stay close to a group of very attractive women. "These youngsters haven't learned that sharing is more fun."

He ignored Ethan's teasing. He'd taken a lot of shit from Ethan, Nick and even Patrick because he wasn't into the sharing thing. He preferred it to be him and one woman, one sweet, little sub. Since he was in no mood to listen to any more crap, he'd change the subject. "Those kids barely look old enough to drink."

"You're showing your age." Ethan patted his shoulder. "You should find some nice, young thing and teach her how to please her master."

"Maybe I will, if any of them show enough originality to dress in something other than red."

"I've got to go and sort out this problem." Ethan slid his phone into his pocket. "I'll find you later. If you find that elusive non-red dress, I'd suggest we share but..." He chuckled as he headed down the stairs, maneuvering through the crowd like he had nowhere to go, when in reality he was heading for the back—the playrooms.

Terry's eyes stopped and lingered on the new hire, Desiree, who was moving around the room, talking and flirting with all the men and some women. She was interesting—exotic and beautiful—but there was a shrewdness behind her eyes that he'd learned a long time ago to avoid. A woman like her had an agenda and she stuck with it, no matter what.

Someone slammed into his back, causing his drink to spill down his front, staining his shirt and suit.

"Oh...oh, I'm so sorry."

He spun around and encountered a red dress and breasts—milky white and lush. The skin would be fragrant and softer than rose petals.

"Oh. Your shirt. Let me get something to wipe that up."

He forced his eyes away from those lovely breasts. Her hair was a rich mahogany. It'd probably hang past her shoulders in waves of curly silk but right now it was piled haphazardly on her head in what had been some kind of elegant style before disobedient strands had escaped their restraint. She looked mussed and damnit, he wanted to be the one to muss her.

"Paper towels? Napkins?" She glanced around and then hurried over to the bar.

She was short and curvy—her body succulent, ripe and he'd bet juicy. She grabbed a stack of napkins and headed for him. Her dress was too tight, like she'd recently gained some weight. He usually went for the tall, athletic types but for some reason his dick had picked this woman.

She returned to his side and dabbed at the wetness on his shirt and jacket as if she actually gave a shit about his clothes. This was no subtle caress, no flirtation—just indifferent efficiency.

"I'm so sorry." She wadded the napkins in her hand, still patting at his clothes.

"You said that already." His words came out gruffer than he'd meant. No one treated him with disinterest. He was a rich, successful, attractive man and she was treating him like a child. He wanted to pull up her—unfortunately, red—dress and fuck her right here. They were at the Club. It wasn't out of the question.

Her hand froze. "Oh." Her large hazel eyes looked startled and then hurt. "Sorry. Ah, excuse me." She headed toward the stairs, dropping the wet napkins in the trash before disappearing in the crowd.

He turned around, so he could see the first floor and waited for her to appear. She hurried across the downstairs room, bumping and stumbling through the crowd. A lone, scared, little rabbit in a room full of predators. She stopped for a moment, scanning the crowd as if searching for someone.

"Who are you looking for, little rabbit?" he mumbled to himself. "A husband? Boyfriend?" He grinned as he lifted his scotch to his lips. "Girlfriend?" He frowned at the empty glass. "You spilled my drink. I'll forgive you, but it's going to cost you." He waved at one of the waitresses. "Everything has a price, little rabbit." As one of the best divorce lawyers in town, he knew that better than anyone.

The waitress brought him another drink. He paid, giving her a large tip before turning to find his little rabbit. He took a sip of the scotch, enjoying the smooth burn and his lush little bunny's journey through La Petite Mort Club. She froze in her tracks, her jaw dropping open as she gazed at a threesome on one of the couches.

The woman was sandwiched between two men, stroking one's cock as the other man fondled her beneath her red dress. The man behind her looked up and said something to the little rabbit. Her face heated and Terry's eyes dropped to her chest. Yep, they were a pretty shade of pink but what he really wanted to know was if the color matched her pussy.

She stumbled away from the threesome, bumping into another man. It was Richard, who stopped her from falling and then immediately let her go, stepping away. She was safe with Richard. As a member of the Club and a gentleman, he knew that safewords were law and consent was absolutely necessary. She said something to him and continued through the Club, disappearing in the crowd.

"You're not getting away that easily." He followed along on the upper floor, keeping her in sight. He had no idea why but he wanted her. Maybe, it was simply because she was different than everyone else here.

He took another sip of his drink. It was obviously the little rabbit's first time at a place like this but she didn't seem eager to participate or interested in watching. She truly seemed to be looking for someone specific—not just someone to fuck. Well, she'd found the latter because he was going to fuck her. In the office he followed his head but at La Petite Mort Club his cock was king.

She headed toward the playrooms. There was no way he was going to miss this. He sauntered down the stairs, grabbing another drink on the way. She wasn't hard to follow. She left a path of irritated people in her wake as she bumped into them and apologized profusely before hurrying forward. Her full, round hips swayed under her tight, red dress that'd seen better days—hem frayed and at least five years out of style. Not that he minded, especially the snug fit of the cloth, but his women were usually much more put together.

They were the CEO types—women who thrived on being in charge. He enjoyed teaching them how much fun turning over control could be. When they were with him, he was their dom, their master and he made sure they loved every second. He told them when to kneel, when to suck, when to spread their legs or ass and when to come. The more power they had in their everyday life the more they craved bowing to his wishes. His little rabbit wouldn't know what power was. She was a hot mess of a woman. Still, his dick wanted her, so his dick would have her.

She was hurrying out of the first playroom when he entered the hallway. Her eyes were huge and her cheeks were on fire. She ducked into the next room and quickly came out— even redder than before.

"Excuse me." He'd offer his assistance in her search. She'd be grateful. He could capitalize on that unless she was looking for her husband or boyfriend. He wasn't in the mood to share. He would, however, allow the other man to watch. He could give the guy some pointers on how to take care of his wife because this woman needed guidance.

"You?" Her eyes narrowed.

That wasn't the reaction he was used to. Women usually purred for him.

"Are you following me?"

"What would you do if I said I was?" He took a step toward her.

"I'd scream. There are bouncers here. I saw them."

Lord, she was cute. "Yes, but if they came running at every little scream they'd die of exhaustion."

As if to emphasis his point, a woman screamed in ecstasy. His little rabbit's face heated and she averted her gaze.

"Who are you looking for?" He skimmed his finger down her cheek. Her skin was as smooth as porcelain but much warmer and softer.

"Ah..." Her breath hitched, making her breasts swell dangerously above her gown.

He could have her out of it in a minute. The skin would be even softer than that on her face. "Did you lose your husband?"

"No." She licked her lips.

There was no way he could let that offer pass. He slowly bent, giving her time to refuse him. He may command his women but he made sure they always wanted it first. Her eyes dropped to his mouth and he couldn't help a slight smirk. She wanted this as much as he did. He moved closer and let his lips rest gently on hers. He'd take it slow, make her yearn for him and then he'd make her obey.

"What are you doing?" She turned her head.

"Kissing you." His lips brushed against her cheek. He wasn't about to lose ground.

"Why?" She turned again, her eyes meeting his.

The confusion in her hazel gaze was as clear as the hideous dress on her gorgeous body. She may remind him of a rabbit but she couldn't be that naive. She had to be in her mid to late thirties.

He should use flowery words—tell her she was beautiful, desirable—but that wasn't him. Blunt was the kindest word to describe him. "Because, I want to."

"You don't even know me."

He was losing ground. The interest in her face was being replaced with disgust. "No, but I know I want you." Damn, he shouldn't have said that.

"Well, too bad." She pushed on his chest and he stepped back, letting her pass.

"This is a sex club, you know." He followed. "If you aren't here for sex, why are you here?"

She spun around. "I'm quite aware of what this place is and just because I don't want you, a stranger to...to"—she waved her hand about—"in the hallway."

He laughed. "We wouldn't be the first. There are people fucking in the main room."

"I know. I saw." Her cheeks heated.

He stepped closer. "You are adorable." He touched a strand of hair that was resting on her shoulder. It was like satin.

8

"I'm a mess." She pulled her hair from his fingers.

"A hot mess. A fiery, hot, sexy mess." He moved closer with every other word. "One I want to fuck, right now."

Her eyes hardened. "Too bad because I don't"—again she waved her hand about—"you know, with strangers in the hallway." She shoved his chest again.

He took a small step back but he wasn't giving up yet. "We can go to a private room."

"No."

Shit. By the look on her face, he'd just made a bigger blunder.

"Let me go." She pushed him again.

Damn. She'd said the worst three words in the English language besides I love you. He moved away, releasing her for the moment. "Sorry."

She harrumphed.

"I made a mistake."

"Yes, you did." She hurried down the hallway but not before he'd seen the look of hurt in her large eyes.

"What the fuck do you want from me? I made a mistake and apologized." He trailed after her.

"I want you to leave me alone. Please. Go away."

He stopped. His little rabbit was running but perhaps, he shouldn't chase. She darted down a hallway toward the hardcore BDSM rooms.

Normally, she'd be fine—embarrassed but fine. Except with all the newbies here, tonight wasn't a normal night. He hurried after her. "Hey, I don't think you want to go—"

"Leave me alone." She walked faster. "I need to find my friend and get out of here."

"Okay, but I don't—"

"Go away." She sounded both mad and as if she were going to cry.

"Suit yourself, but I warned you."

She strode into the closest room. He should leave. Let her find out that he wasn't the worst thing in a place like this, not in a long shot, but his feet followed her. She was his little rabbit. He'd found her. No one else was going to enjoy her until he'd had his taste.

"Vicky? Vicky? Are you in here?"

He stepped into the room, staying in the shadows. She was looking around in the dark for her friend. It only took a moment for one of the six guys to notice the little rabbit who'd stumbled into their den.

"Shit," he mumbled. Not one of those guys was a regular.

CHAPTER 2: Maggie

That man was an ass. Maggie had never met a guy like him, but he fit every preconceived notion she had of rich, handsome men—tall, arrogant, dark haired, entitled, in excellent shape and his suit had to cost a fortune. She needed to find Vicky and get out of this place. She wasn't a prude but the things they were doing in here—in public—were indecent, immoral. She should be disgusted but she wasn't. She was flushed and not only from embarrassment. It'd been over a year since her divorce and she was lonely.

"Hey there, sweetheart." A tall guy stepped forward, smiling at her breasts.

"Hello. Have you seen…"

A woman was bent over a wooden horse, naked except for a black scarf around her eyes. Her hands were tied together in front and her legs tied to two of the horse's legs. Several men surrounded her, all in various stages of undress. A man, wearing assless chaps and a mask, stood behind her holding a paddle. By the color of the woman's butt, he'd used it…a lot.

"We have a new toy," said one of the other men. "I can't wait to see those titties swing when we spank her."

"I want to fuck her so hard they bounce," said the tall guy who'd first greeted her.

"Oh...oh...no. I'm sorry." She stumbled backward but the men shifted, blocking her route to the door.

"Don't run away, darling," said the tall man. "You'll love it. We'll make sure." He grabbed her shoulders, twisting her so she was staring right at the woman in the center of the room. "Watch Renee. See how much fun she's having."

The man in the chaps slapped Renee's ass with the paddle and she screamed. He caressed her skin, letting his fingers slip between her legs and stroke her pussy.

"Yes...please," moaned Renee.

Maggie's breath hitched in her chest as the other woman writhed against the man's fingers. She'd never imagined being spanked could bring pleasure.

"See. You'll like it." The tall man's breath was hot in her ear—the heavy scent of alcohol making her turn away. "Watch while he fucks her and then we'll all fuck her." He began pushing Maggie toward another wooden horse.

"What?" Oh, no. This was not for her.

"Don't worry. We'll fuck you too."

"No, please. Let me go." She tried to pull free but his fingers dug into her arms. "I don't want to do this." Her stomach roiled. She was going to puke.

"You know the rules, boys," said someone from near the door.

She knew that voice. It was the man from the hallway. "Please, help me."

"Yeah, we know the rules. Everyone has to want it." The tall man yanked her to his side and squeezed her ass. "She does."

"I don't. I don't want this." She elbowed him in the stomach but he only tightened his grip.

"Don't lie, bitch. You want it. You came in here and walked right over to us."

"I came in here by accident. I was looking for my friend. I couldn't see what you were doing." It sounded stupid even to her, but the room was dark and she'd heard a moan and had thought Vicky might be in trouble.

"We'd love to be your friends." The tall man pulled her closer. "Wouldn't we?"

The other men chimed in with agreement.

"We ain't opposed to one more." The tall guy turned to the man from the hallway. "But you go last."

Dear God, she was going to be gang raped. She had to get out of there. "Let me go." She shoved at the man, but he was too strong.

"You heard her." The hallway man's voice was low and dangerous. "She is not consenting. You know the rules."

The man holding her looked at the tall, dark stranger. "Fine. Take her. Bitch ain't worth the trouble." He shoved her toward the hallway man.

She stumbled forward, tripping over the tall guy's foot. The stranger moved fast like a cat, catching her against his body long enough to steady her, before taking her arm and pushing her behind him.

"She's too fat anyway." The tall guy walked toward the restrained woman.

It shouldn't hurt. She didn't know this man or like what she did know about him, but the words, so similar to her ex-husband's, stung.

"Renee, it's Terry. Are you okay?" asked the man from the hallway.

"Fabulous," she purred as the man with the paddle trailed kisses across her pink ass.

"Good." Terry grabbed Maggie's arm. "Let's go."

She almost had to run to keep up with his long strides. He dropped his hold as soon as they stepped into the hallway. He closed the door, shutting out the danger and Maggie's knees buckled. That could've been so bad.

"Hey, you okay?" Terry touched her arm, but it was with concern not force.

"Thank you." She blinked back tears but they slipped out anyway. All she'd wanted was a night out—to be a woman for a few hours, not a mother, not a hostess and not an unwanted and unloved wife, ex-wife.

"Ah, hell." He took her hand and started down the hallway.

"Where are you taking me?" She pulled against his grip. She'd just gotten out of a situation. She wasn't about to jump into another one.

He stopped, giving her a disgusted look. "I saved you from being raped and you still don't trust me?"

"I…ah…" It did sound a little unappreciative the way he said it.

"I don't force women. Ever." He squeezed her hand which she hadn't even thought about removing from his grasp. "I need to report their behavior to Ethan."

"Ethan?"

"The owner. I don't want anyone else accidentally encountering them."

"The owner will do something?"

"Of course. This is a reputable club. There is no rape here. Rape fantasies, sure, but not rape."

"A respectable sex club? Right." She'd heard about these kinds of places but the real thing was so much worse. "Those guys were so respectful."

"Those guys are not members and never will be."

"You're a member." She should've known. He may have saved her but he'd also tried to have sex with her in this very hallway.

"Yes, I am." Pride filled his tone. "And I assure you, no member would ever do anything like those guys were going to do to you. It isn't allowed. Ever." He tugged on her hand. "I really need to speak with Ethan."

"I-I need to find my friend." She didn't want to wander around alone but Vicky could be hurt or in a bad situation like she'd been.

"We can do that too. Ethan will find your friend and you can wait in one of the back rooms."

Her breath hitched in her throat. That was where he'd said they could go to have sex in private.

He sighed as if weary of this conversation. "You turned me down. You were almost raped. I'm not going to attack you. Trust me."

She nodded, following him down the hallway and hoping she wasn't making the biggest mistake of her life.

CHAPTER 3: Terry

Terry followed his frightened little rabbit inside one of the private suites and closed the door behind them.

"This is where..." She looked around the room, eyes wide.

Ethan didn't do anything half-assed, including decorating these rooms. The carpet was plush and brown with hints of blue to match the walls. The furniture was a solid, light-colored wood, a refreshing break from the darker décor of the club.

"There's no bed?" She looked at him her face pale as a hint of a blush crept into her cheeks. "Not that we were..." Her hands fluttered in her nervousness.

"Believe me, you made that perfectly clear." But he had every intention of changing her mind—not tonight, but soon.

"I didn't mean it."

He raised his brow. Maybe, tonight would work.

"No. I...that's not..." She took a deep breath. "We aren't going to, you know, but I didn't mean to be rude."

"I don't mind." He chuckled. She was beyond adorable. "I'm almost always rude."

"No." She reached out as if to touch him but stopped, her fingers only a breath away from his arm. "You saved me. Thank you."

"You're welcome, but I shouldn't have had to. Which reminds me." He pulled his cell phone from his pocket and texted Ethan, sliding it back into his jacket when he was done. "Please, have a seat." He motioned to one of the chairs by the couch and then pointed at the door near the bar. "That should be the bathroom and there"—he nodded at the door across from them—"should be the bedroom...with the bed."

"Oh." She blushed, looking anywhere but at him.

It was a promising sign. He moved to the bar. His little rabbit was shy and flustered, a little frightened after her ordeal but she was attracted to him which meant, he'd have her. It may take some persuading but he loved a challenge. "Drink?" He poured himself a scotch on the rocks.

"No. Thank you." She was sitting on a chair, her entire body stiff, but her eyes kept darting his way and skimming over him in a fleeting caress.

She might not be as much of a challenge as he'd thought and that was excellent. He was in the market for a new sub and she'd be fun to mold. He poured her some wine and carried it to her.

He sat on the chair across from hers, putting his drink on the nearby table. He leaned forward, taking her hand. It was small and cold. He wrapped it around the wine glass. "This will help with your nerves." He kept a hold of her, his heat warming her chilled flesh.

"Okay." Her gaze was on their hands but she didn't attempt to pull free. "Thank you."

"You're welcome." He continued to stare at her for one long moment. If she looked up, he'd kiss her and take her mind off her near rape.

"I-I don't know what I would've done if you hadn't..." Her hand began to tremble. She looked up at him and he could've sworn his heart wrenched in his chest. She was so vulnerable, helpless and scared.

"Come here." He took the glass from her and set it by his before tugging on her hand.

"Wh-what are you doing?" There was a hitch of panic in her voice.

"Trust me." His hands went to her waist. "I'm not going to do anything but hold you." He lifted her, placing her on his lap.

"Let me go." She struggled.

"I won't touch you. I swear." He lifted his hands. Forcing her wouldn't gain her trust and he needed her to trust him if she were going to submit to him.

"You're touching me now." She glanced down. "Just about everywhere."

"That's not what I meant and you know it."

"Yeah. Well..."

When she didn't move, he wanted to grin like a fool but instead he wrapped an arm around her waist and pulled her head to his shoulder. "You're safe now. No one can hurt you." He'd protect her. All she had to do was let him.

"I don't even know you." She stiffened, as if having second thoughts about their situation.

He couldn't allow that. He loosened his hold a little and she relaxed. Okay, so that was how she worked. It might take a while to get her to bend to his wishes, but he was patient and determined. In the end, she'd submit. "I'm Terry."

"I'm Maggie." She relaxed a little more.

She was soft and lush and smelled good—vanilla, woman and strawberries from her shampoo. Delicious. Later she'd be his to taste, but for right now….He grabbed her wine and handed it to her. "Drink."

She took a sip and then another. He smiled against the top of her head. She was a fast study. She'd be obeying his every whim soon.

CHAPTER 4: Maggie

Maggie should get up and sit on her own chair, but her body melted against Terry's warmth and strength. She needed this closeness for just a moment. The terror from earlier still rolled through her in shockwaves and it'd been so long since she'd been able to count on a man for anything. Not that she could count on him for more than this small comfort.

"Relax."

She let him take the glass from her hand again. He put it on the table and pulled her head to his chest. His heart beat strong and steady. She missed this closeness. She'd been divorced for over a year but even before that David had barely touched her, except when he'd wanted sex. This was different. Terry didn't seem to want anything from her.

"You're cold. Probably, shock." His hand ran up and down her arm.

"I'm fine." She wasn't but she could be if only time would stop for a while. She'd been so worried lately, so alone, and she still was. She took a deep breath. "I should move."

"Why?" He seemed genuinely confused.

"I don't know you." She sat up and blushed when she felt a bulge against her thigh. Apparently, more than her comfort was on his mind. "I'm not in the habit of being held by strange men."

"Why did you come to a sex club?" His hand was on her hip now, holding her in place and he was growing beneath her leg. "Unless you know someone here, besides that friend you're looking for, I assume you came for sex with a strange man...or woman."

"What? No. I'm not...I'm not into women." She shoved at his hand and he dropped his arms, not even trying to keep her on his lap. She wasn't disappointed. Truly, she wasn't. She stood. A guy like him wouldn't actually be attracted to her.

He was older, maybe early to mid-forties, distinguished, in great physical shape and handsome but not in a pretty-boy way. He had dark hair that was graying at the temples and a man's face with a five o'clock shadow and heavy brow and jaw, but his lips were sensual and his eyes a warm, dark brown.

"Then a strange man was your goal." He smiled, his gaze roaming over her face and down across her breasts like a caress. "I'd be more than happy to help, whenever you're ready."

"I didn't come here for that." She started pacing. "I didn't know this was a sex club."

There was a knock on the door. "Terry, it's Ethan."

Terry walked to the door, moving with a fluid grace that bespoke confidence and strength. He was a large man—broad shoulders and tall. Her heart skipped a beat. He'd probably be big down there too. She closed her eyes counting to five. She would not think about that. It'd been a long time since she'd had sex but she wasn't going to do it with a stranger, even one who looked like him. She did not have one-night stands, no matter how tempting. "I'm not like that."

Terry opened the door and turned toward her. "I'm sorry,

what did you say?"

"Nothing." Her face heated. "I was talking to myself."

Another man walked into the room and her mouth dropped open. She had to consciously command her jaw to close. Terry was attractive but this man was drop-dead gorgeous. Ethan had sandy blonde hair and blue eyes like the ocean, but he was more than handsome. There was a sophisticated elegance about him mixed with danger and temptation.

"Hi, I'm Ethan." He walked over to her and held out his hand. "I'm so sorry for what happened."

"Thank you." The words came out breathless and flirty. Good lord, what was wrong with her?

Ethan's eyes sparkled and she almost missed the quick trip they took to her bosom.

"Did you take care of them?" Terry's voice was clipped.

"Of course." Ethan glanced at the other man his brow wrinkled with confusion. "They've been evicted from the Club and will never be allowed back."

Terry moved to her side, taking her arm. "Maggie, why don't you sit and tell Ethan what happened." He led her to a chair and stood next to her.

Ethan's eyes gleamed with amusement.

"This is funny to you?" She couldn't help it. He was either laughing at the situation she'd been in or he was laughing at her. She was a mess—hair, makeup and dress.

"No." Ethan immediately sobered. "Not at all. I'm sorry."

She almost asked why he was amused but decided that she didn't want to hear him flounder for an excuse. To be honest, she'd been a partial mess before she'd left her house. The babysitter had been late and Isabella, her oldest, had wanted to help with her hair. She'd had to wear an old dress because she couldn't afford a new one and it was too tight. She hadn't quite lost the baby weight even though it'd been almost two years since she'd had little Davy. The final touch was when Peter had hugged her, smearing a bit of vanilla ice cream on her hem. She hadn't changed because she didn't have anything else. She was nothing but a frumpy fool to men like these.

"I take the safety of everyone at the Club very seriously." Ethan sat on the chair across from her. "Tell me what happened."

"You said you took care of it. Kicked them out." Panic clawed at her throat. She didn't want to relive it by talking about it.

"Yes, but I need to know. Why did you go in there? Into that part of the Club?"

"So, this is my fault?" Unbelievable. She'd almost been gang raped and she was to blame because she'd wandered into the wrong room.

"Of course not, don't be a fool," said Terry

"Now, I'm a fool?" She stood. "I've had enough insults for one night."

"Sit down." Terry's voice was firm.

She had no idea why, but her legs bent and she sat.

"Good girl." Terry's lips curled in smug satisfaction.

"I'm not a girl." She wanted to slap that smirk from his handsome face.

"No doubt about that." His eyes roamed over her body, making her skin tingle, before he turned and grabbed another chair. He placed it on the other side of hers and sat.

"I didn't mean to imply you were at fault." Ethan's voice was smooth and as calming as a warm breeze. "I just like to have all the facts."

"Oh. Okay. I understand that." She took a deep, shaky breath. "I...I..." She really didn't want to talk about those men and what almost happened in that room.

Ethan reached for her hand but Terry grabbed it first, causing Ethan's eyes to almost explode with humor. Something was going on between the two men. They were probably playing some sick game with her, like in the movies when the handsome guy dates the plain girl on a bet.

"Why don't you start with why you came here tonight?" Terry shot Ethan a dirty look.

"I didn't know what kind of club this was until I got inside. My sister-in-law invited—"

"You're married?" asked Terry.

"Divorced. She's my ex-sister-in-law but we're still friends. Vicky invited me to go out with her tonight." Her hand tightened around his. "You have to find her. I was looking for her when I stumbled into that room. She might be..." Vicky might be getting hurt or raped and she'd been sitting here snuggling in Terry's arms. She was a horrible person.

"Don't worry. We'll find her," said Ethan. "Terry mentioned something about your friend in his text. I have security checking all the rooms to ensure no one is there unless they want to be."

"Thank you." She wanted to melt against the seat but instead squeezed Terry's hand.

"Now, what does your friend look like?" Ethan pulled out his phone.

"She's about my age, slender, blonde hair."

"Straight or curly? Long or short?" Ethan was typing the information as she spoke.

"Straight hair and it's about shoulder length."

"What was she was wearing?"

"I'll bet it was red," muttered Terry.

"I don't know. We were meeting here." She glanced at Terry. Did he not like red? Her gaze dropped to her old, tight, red dress.

"Okay." Ethan stood and walked across the room. "We'll start searching for her. You wait here." He paused. "Terry can keep you company." He opened the door. "What's her last name?"

"Givens."

"Vicky Givens?" asked Ethan.

"Yes."

"Thanks. I'll be back soon." Ethan smiled and left.

CHAPTER 5: Terry

Terry stared at the closed door. Something was going on. Ethan was excellent at hiding his true thoughts but he'd known the man for years and as a lawyer, he'd learned to see behind the masks people wore.

"If something happened to her..." Maggie stood and began to pace. "David is going to blame me."

He grabbed her wine glass from the table and went to the bar. He was thankful for the distraction, especially since she was such a hot mess. He had no idea how it'd happened but her hair was even more mussed than earlier. New, thick strands had slipped free from their restraint and rested on her shoulders. His fingers itched to feel that satiny softness, but it wasn't the time, not yet. He filled her glass with wine and walked over to her. "Relax. Your friend will be fine."

"How do you know?" She accepted the glass from him. "I wouldn't have been if you hadn't..." She gulped half of her drink.

He took her arm, enjoying the softness of her body as he led her to the chair. "Sit." He struggled to keep the satisfaction from his face when she immediately obeyed. She didn't realize it but she was a natural submissive. He couldn't wait to train her for his pleasure and hers.

"She may be in trouble too. Like I was." She stared up at him, her eyes huge and filled with worry. She was beyond adorable.

"I doubt that."

"You don't know."

"Let's look at the facts, okay?" She nodded and he sat across from her, letting his knees brush against hers. "She invited you here, right?"

"Yeah." She took a sip of her wine.

"You got into trouble because you didn't realize what kind of place this was."

"Yes, but—"

"If you'd known what went on in the playrooms, would you have gone there?"

"No. Absolutely not."

He smiled slightly. He'd enjoy taking her in every one of them and showing her the pleasures to be had. "Since this event was only open to members, their guests and some others who have applied to be members, your friend, Vicky, has to be familiar with the Club. She'll avoid those rooms, unless that's what she's into."

"She wouldn't want...." She took a much larger sip of her wine.

He leaned back in his seat, enjoying the slight flush creeping into her cheeks. His eyes dipped for a quick glance. The tops of her breasts were a shade or so lighter than her face. He took a sip of his scotch, grimacing slightly. The ice had melted and it was weak and watery.

"She's not...I mean, she's a little wild but she'd never want to do anything like that." She finished her drink.

Terry carried his glass to the bar, dumping the contents in the sink before refilling it and grabbing the bottle of wine.

"I'm sure she didn't know what type of place this was either. Someone must've tricked her. She'd never want to do..."

He refilled her glass and sat. "You can't be that innocent. You *were* married."

"What has that got to do with this?" She was in a huff now and it was a glorious sight. Her rapid breathing caused her large breasts to jiggle in her too tight dress.

His dick started to rise, wanting to get its own look at the wonder of her tits. "This is a sex club. Married people have sex."

"Not like that."

"No wonder you got divorced."

Her mouth dropped open and her eyes widened. Oh, his dick was paying full attention now. Her lips were lush and red and would wrap around his cock so nicely.

"That was a terrible thing to say." She almost huffed her breasts out of her dress.

"I told you I was rude." He leaned forward. "But if all you and your husband did was fuck missionary style it's probably why he left." He took a sip of his drink, his eyes roving over her mouth, wondering what it'd feel like, taste like. "I'm assuming it was he who left."

"That's none of your business. None of this is any of your business." She put her drink down on the nearby table. "I think I'd prefer to wait by myself."

"Too bad." He grinned. "I'm not leaving you alone. Who knows what other mischief you'll find?"

"I'm not an idiot. I'm not going to do anything but wait here for Ethan." She was sitting as stiff as if she were strapped to a post, but her voice had held a hint of breathlessness when she'd said Ethan's name.

"All the same, I'll keep you company." He took another sip of his drink, tamping down his irritation at her and himself. He'd never been the jealous type. Ethan liked innocent, young women. He liked experienced women who thought they knew what they wanted, but this time, this innocent woman was his.

"I don't need your kind of company."

"The last time you told me to go away you ended up in a situation that could've been very serious."

"Yes, I did." She frowned, as if in pain. "Thank you again for saving me." She forced a smile. "Why don't we talk about something else?"

She was a pleaser by nature. Terry liked pleasers. "Who's David?"

"Why?" She was getting defensive again.

But he'd break down every wall until she learned to trust him completely. Then, they'd play. "You said David would blame you if anything happened to Vicky."

"Oh. Right. I did." She took a sip of her drink. "He's my ex. Vicky's older brother."

"When I got divorced, I stopped having anything to do with all of my ex's family." It'd been hard and lonely. They'd been his family too for more than twelve years.

"Vicky and I were friends before David and I married. That's how I met him."

"Still. Uncomfortable." Cutting all ties was hard but best in the long run.

She shrugged but her eyes sparkled. Mischievous Maggie was a sight to behold—red, lush lips, breasts a man could be happy being smothered by, and hazel eyes eager and interested. Too bad she wasn't looking at his dick.

"If you think my marriage failed due to"—her hand fluttered—"bedroom issues, what about yours? Same reason?" Her face was red now, but she held his gaze.

"Hardly. I wasn't a member here then but we did more than fuck missionary style."

"I forgot you were a member." She glanced down. "Do you come here a lot?"

"Yes." He grinned. "I come here very often."

She looked up at him, her brow wrinkled in confusion. Terry knew the exact moment she understood his double entendre. Her cheeks heated and for one glorious second her eyes dipped to his crotch. He'd love to unzip his pants and let her get a good look, but she wasn't quite ready for that.

"That's not what I meant." She took the last sip of her wine.

"I know. That's why it was funny." He grabbed the bottle and leaned over to fill her glass.

"I shouldn't." She put her hand on the top.

"Did you drive?"

"No. I took an Uber. Vicky was going to take me home."

He moved her hand and filled her glass. "Then drink up."

"I really shouldn't. I have to be up early."

"One more glass won't kill you." He let his knee brush against hers and her eyes immediately went to their legs. Good. She felt the attraction too.

She picked up the glass and shifted, leaning back in her

seat and breaking the connection with his leg.

You can run, little rabbit but you won't escape. He took another drink, savoring the chase. Would he taste his little rabbit tonight or would she make him work for it? He couldn't decide which would be more fun. Fucking her now would ease the ache in his groin but waiting…That was the sweetest torture.

"What do you do for a living?" she asked.

"Safe topic."

"I thought so." She smiled over her glass.

It was the first real smile he'd seen and it was like a massive jolt to his dick. He didn't want to wait. He wanted her now. His hand tightened around his drink. "I'm a lawyer."

"Oh, that's nice."

He shrugged. It was a job and he was damn good at it. "You?"

"I'm a hostess at Outback." She glanced away.

She was hiding something, but he'd ferret out all her secrets. Knowing everything about her was the only way to wring every spark of pleasure from her body. "I'll have to start eating there more often."

Her smile was fleeting but bright, like the sun peeking through the clouds on a dismal day. "Why were you following me?" She held up her hand. "I'm not complaining. If you hadn't been there…I was just wondering why?"

"Do you really want to know?" He leaned forward until he was a few inches from her. "And before you answer, I need to warn you that I don't sugarcoat anything. Not for any reason. I've already told you that I'm rude but I've also been called crass and brutally honest." He took a deep breath. "This is the only warning you'll get. Don't ask me any questions unless you want my honest answer because that's the only kind I give."

She nodded and took a sip of her drink. She seemed to draw some courage from it because she repeated, "Why were you following me?"

"Because I want to fuck you."

CHAPTER 6: Maggie

Maggie almost dropped her drink. She'd never had a man, even her husband, talk to her like that.

Terry leaned closer. She should move but his dark eyes held her in place, mesmerizing her like a rabbit facing a snake. She could smell the light scent of scotch on his breath and his musky, masculine cologne. Her eyes dropped to his lips, sensual especially paired with his strong cheek bones and five o'clock shadow.

"You're giving me all sorts of ideas." He touched her chin, his finger warm and rough as he closed her mouth.

She hadn't realized that her mouth had been hanging open. She must be as red as a tomato because he laughed and leaned back against his seat

"No comment?" His eyes sparkled with humor.

"No one has ever spoken to me like that." Usually, she let things slide, tried to see the good in everything and everyone, but this attractive, sophisticated, arrogant man thought he was better than her because he was rich and worldly.

"Shame."

She almost sputtered. "It is not. It's rude and…"

"Crass?" He laughed but quickly sobered. "Like I promised, brutally honest." His gaze lingered on her lips before dropping to her breasts.

Most men pretended not to stare at her chest, but not him. His dark eyes sparkled like they could see through the cloth. She wanted to fan herself or hide, or maybe, pull the top of her dress down so he could get a good look. *And a taste.* She blinked. No, she did not want that. She didn't even know this man.

"Why did you come to the Club?" His gaze lifted to hers.

"I told you. I didn't know what this place was."

"Yes, but you went out tonight looking for something."

"Not this. Not a relationship."

"Then you came to the right place." This time his smile was wide and god help her he was even better looking.

"I wasn't looking for"—she lowered her voice—"sex either."

His smile shifted becoming more smug as one side of his mouth lifted in a smirk. "Then what were you looking for if not a relationship and not sex? Conversation?"

"Well, no. I don't know." She took a gulp of the wine. What had she expected to find tonight? She really didn't have time for a relationship, not with work and the kids, but she was lonely. "I'm not the kind of woman who has one-night stands."

"Good because one night with you won't be enough." His voice had grown darker and richer.

"Oh." That was the nicest thing she'd heard from a man in years.

"I'll need more time than that to teach you how to please me."

34

Her mouth dropped open again and when his dark eyes landed on her lips, she snapped her jaw shut, making her teeth clank together.

The ass laughed as he leaned forward. "We can have an arrangement." His hand slipped behind her neck. It was warm and strong, making her want to dissolve into him. "I promise. You'll enjoy every minute."

His mouth came down on hers, gentle and coaxing. His tongue played along the crease of her lips but she couldn't let him in. She hadn't kissed anyone but her husband in over ten years. She had no idea how to kiss anyone else. It'd been too long. What if she were a bad kisser?

His lips moved to her ear and down her neck as his other hand cupped her cheek. Her head rested against his palm. He was an excellent kisser, his lips warm and coaxing. He smelled so good, cologne, fabric softener and him. It'd been so long since she'd been touched or held by a man. He nibbled her ear and she gasped, reaching for him, no longer worried about anything but touching him. Her fingers tangled in the lapels of his jacket. His chest was strong beneath her knuckles and the heat from his body made her want to wrap around him and soak in his warmth.

His lips found a spot behind her ear and a throaty moan slipped from her. Before she could breathe his mouth was on hers, his tongue sliding inside. The faint taste of scotch was dark and delicious and she couldn't get enough.

His hand moved to the hem of her dress, slipping underneath. She should stop him, but she didn't want to. He was right. This was what she'd been looking for—to feel desired, wanted, sexy.

"Ahem. Excuse me."

She gasped and broke from the kiss, pushing on his chest but it was like moving a mountain with a feather.

"Go away, Ethan," Terry said against her neck, his fingers still trailing farther up her thigh. "Come back in an hour."

"Stop it." She slapped at his hand, her face flushing from passion and embarrassment.

"Shit." Terry straightened his eyes on her legs.

She started to tug her dress down, but he bent, his lips brushing against the exposed flesh of her thigh and his tongue darting out for a quick taste that made her insides throb and her thighs drop open a little more. He smirked as he leaned back in his chair.

Her hands trembled and her breathing was rapid as she pulled her hem down, covering her legs. Terry's dark eyes were like a weight as she tried to look anywhere but at either of the men.

"Ah Terry, can I speak with you?" Ethan nodded at the door.

"Did you find Vicky?" She was a terrible person. Once again, she'd forgotten about her friend.

"No. She's not here," said Ethan.

"Not here? She has to be here."

"Terry." Ethan's head snapped toward the door.

"Did something happen to her?"

"Nothing happened to her." Ethan sighed. "Vicky Givens is not allowed here any longer."

"What?" That meant that Vicky used to come here. That meant that Vicky knew exactly what kind of place this was.

"Your friend used to be a regular, but I had to cancel her

membership."

"When did you cancel?" Her stomach felt like she'd eaten a boulder.

"Six months ago."

"Did she know?" This had to be a mistake.

"Yes. I told her personally." Ethan walked toward her. "She also knew that she couldn't sneak inside. She must've convinced another member to put you down as a guest. Don't worry. I'll find out who."

She nodded, tears forming at the back of her eyes. She'd thought they were still friends. She'd believed Vicky had gotten over the divorce but she'd been wrong. She gulped down her drink. Vicky had done this on purpose.

"I'm sorry." Ethan walked over to her.

"I was almost raped. Vicky couldn't have wanted that to happen. She couldn't have." She and Vicky had been friends for years. The other woman couldn't hate her. The divorce wasn't even her fault.

"I'm very sorry about that. About all of it." Ethan took her hand. "Come. Let me take you home."

"I'll take her." Terry stood, snatching her hand from Ethan.

CHAPTER 7: Terry

Terry led Maggie to his car and held the door while she climbed inside. So much for a night of sex. She was a mess. He got into the driver's side. "What's your address?"

She rattled it off and he input it into the GPS. She stared out the window, shoulders slumped and the sparkle long gone from her tear-filled eyes. She looked like her entire world had collapsed and he had no idea how to fix it.

He pulled out of the parking lot. "I'm sorry." It was the best he had.

She sniffled.

His foot pushed down on the gas. He was great with stubborn women, angry women, flustered women but not crying women. He always said the wrong thing and made everything worse.

"Not your fault." She used part of her sleeve to dab at her eyes.

"No, but I'm sorry anyway." There, that wasn't too bad.

"Don't be." She sat up straighter. "At least, I now know what kind of person she really is. Although, I'm sure she didn't think I'd almost be raped." She shook her head. "No. Vicky wouldn't have done that."

"Stop, okay. This woman, this friend, tricked you into going to a sex club. She had to know you'd look for her and that meant she had to, at least, assume you'd go into the playrooms." The words came out harsher than he'd meant.

"I guess, but that doesn't mean she thought men like them would be there."

"Still. She put you at risk, leaving you there alone." His fist tightened on the steering wheel. Maggie was sweet and basically innocent. She should never be in the Club alone, with him was a different story.

"You said things like that didn't happen at the Club. You said everyone understood who wanted to...you know and who didn't."

"Jesus, you can't even say the word, can you?" He glanced at her.

"Yes, I can, but I don't see the reason."

"I don't believe you."

She was getting flustered but at least she wasn't ready to cry. "Fine. Have sex. Are you happy now?"

"That's not the word I meant."

"Well, that's the only word I'm going to say." She crossed her arms over her chest.

"I'll take that as a challenge." He couldn't wait to make her pant for him, beg him to fuck her.

"It wasn't." She turned toward the window, sad again.

"Come on, say it."

"No."

"Please."

She glanced at him. "No." But her tone was amused. "I'm

not saying the f-word."

"You owe me."

"Now, I owe you for saving me?"

"Of course." He grinned. "Everything has a price and I want to hear you say fuck."

"Too bad. Tonight, you're not going to get what you want."

"You're right about that." He made sure she saw his eyes rake over her and he swore she shivered. "You know, when we get to your place, we can finish what we started before Ethan interrupted."

"I-I don't think so."

"Indecision. I'll take that as a yes."

She laughed. "It's not. Trust me, we're not doing anything at my house."

"There's a nice hotel right up the street."

She laughed harder. "Going to a hotel with you is not a good idea."

"But it'll be fun." He stopped at a light and he leaned toward her. "Don't you want to be naughty? I bet your ex is being naughty. If he left you, he probably already has another woman."

Her shoulders drooped and tears formed in her eyes.

Damn, he'd blown it again. "I'm sorry."

"You should be."

He hadn't expected that. He almost snapped that it was the truth, but instead gritted his teeth and drove in silence. She sniffled and he stepped on the gas. He had no idea how to stop her from crying, so getting her home was the next best thing. He followed the GPS and pulled into a driveway at a nice house in a nice neighborhood.

"Thank you for the ride."

"I'll give you a ride anytime. Any kind of ride you want."

"Stop. Please." She got out of the car. "I really...just can't." She closed the door and headed up the driveway.

"Wait." He hurried after her, catching her on the front porch. He wasn't giving up yet. "I'd like to see you again." He'd like to see her naked and bent over his lap.

She sighed. It was sad and weary. "I appreciate everything you've done for me, but I don't have time for anything else in my life." She opened the door and slipped inside.

Damn, he loved a challenge.

CHAPTER 8: Terry

The next evening, Terry knocked twice and walked into Ethan's office, heading straight to the bar in the back room.

"What are you doing here?" Ethan was stretched out on the couch watching the Club through the monitors. "Do you need a room or something?"

"No. Why would you ask that?" He grabbed the scotch and poured himself a drink.

Ethan held his brandy snifter up for a refill. "Because you found a sub last night."

Terry filled Ethan's glass before plopping his large frame onto one of the big chairs. "Hardly."

"What happened?" Ethan sat up.

"Besides you interrupting?" He was still a little pissed about that. Ethan could've stepped inside and discreetly left. The bastard had probably wanted to join.

"Sorry. I didn't think you'd be making a move."

"Oh? Why?" She wasn't exactly his type but he'd made it clear that he was interested in her.

"She'd almost been raped."

"Oh. Yeah. That." He took a sip of his drink. "You know what they say. When you fall off a bike, it's best to get right back on."

"You're an ass." Ethan laughed.

Terry chuckled. "Never said I wasn't."

"So, what happened?"

"Nothing."

"Nothing? Really? You struck out?" Ethan grinned.

"For now." He had no intentions of letting his little rabbit get away for good.

"You're going after her?" Ethan studied him. "I haven't seen you chase a woman in years."

"And you won't this time either." He did not pursue women.

"Then, you don't want her?"

"I do, but she'll come to me." He wasn't sure how he'd accomplish that, but a little peek into her life and he'd find some way he could assist her besides in the bedroom.

"Really? What are you going to do? Sue her for something?"

"If I have to." He smiled.

"Hmm."

"Don't start. I'm telling you, she wants me."

"She just doesn't know it." Ethan rolled his eyes. "Now, you sound like Nick did."

"Don't ever say that." He tried to keep a straight face but failed. He and Nick always bickered but the young guy was like a somewhat estranged brother to him. "And this is different because she knows she wants me, but she's scared."

"Good instincts, that one."

"Fuck you."

The phone rang and Ethan answered it. "Who?" He smirked at Terry. "Send her up."

"Who's here?" Terry was nervous. Ethan had that same look of victory in his eyes as when he'd bet on something with bad odds and won.

"You'll see." Ethan stood and made a production of straightening his clothes and hair.

"Who is it, the fucking Queen or something?" He didn't like this. As a lawyer, he wanted to know the answers before the questions were asked.

There was a knock on the door. Ethan strode over and opened it. "Come in."

Terry followed him out of the back room and almost groaned. It was Maggie. She was dressed in her Outback uniform and she looked delicious with the black pants and white button-down shirt. He wanted to unbutton it and kiss that soft skin until he found her breasts. They'd be warm and smooth, softer than satin, and her nipples would be succulent.

"Oh. Hi." She smiled at Terry. "I didn't think you'd be here."

"Really?" She'd come to be with Ethan. Not terribly surprising. All women wanted Ethan but this time it sucked. He'd wanted the little innocent.

"But, I had hoped that since you were a member, Ethan would know how to find you." She walked over to him, carrying a brown grocery bag.

"So, you came to find me, not Ethan." He sent his friend his own look of victory.

"Yeah. This is for you." She held the bag out to him. "I was less than gracious last night and I wanted to thank you."

"You already thanked me." He would've rather she'd thanked him with a fuck but her words would have to suffice for now.

"Not enough. I really appreciate you helping me." Her eyes went to the bag. "I know this isn't much but..."

He took the bag and opened it. He pulled out the large container and removed the lid.

"Damn. That smells good." Ethan moved a little closer.

"I didn't know what kind of cookies you liked so I made chocolate chip—most people like those—sugar, peanut butter and oatmeal raisin."

The container was almost overflowing. Terry couldn't help but stare at all the goodies. "You made these?"

"Yeah." A slight blush crept across her cheeks.

Immediately, his eyes dropped to her breasts but tonight those lovelies were concealed by clothes. "Thank you." He hadn't had homemade cookies since he was a kid.

"Like I said, it isn't much but—"

"No. I mean it. Thank you." He put them aside and moved toward her. "Would you like a drink?" His little rabbit had returned and he wasn't about to let her scurry away again.

"You're welcome and no. I have to get home."

"You could stay for one." He smiled, letting his eyes roam down her frame.

She backed away, more heat filling her cheeks. "Really, I can't. Thank you, though."

Always so polite, his little rabbit. He couldn't wait to make her beg him for his cock. He'd make sure she said both please and thank you. "I'll walk you out."

"Oh. No." She glanced at Ethan. "I didn't mean to interrupt."

"Ethan won't mind." He moved toward her slowly and purposefully. He wasn't letting her escape without at least having a taste of her.

"Me?" mumbled Ethan around a cookie. "No. Go. Have fun." He shoved another cookie in his mouth. "These are fabulous."

"See?" Terry almost purred as he continued to the door.

"You don't have to." She was ready to bolt. "I can get back to my car by myself."

"I'm sure you can, but"—he leaned close to her ear—"I want to escort you."

"Oh. Okay." She stared up at him, waiting. She was so ready to follow his lead.

"After you." He opened the door.

"Of course. Thank you."

They walked down the hallway and into the elevator. He stayed close to her, his shoulder almost brushing against hers, building the anticipation for when he did touch her. He pressed the button for the ground floor. "Did you park in the garage?"

"No, the parking lot."

He nodded.

"You really don't have to do this."

The quaver in her voice was music to his ears. There was no way she thought he'd hurt her which meant the only reason for her nervousness was attraction. It was time to show her that she had no reason to fear her feelings for him. He turned toward her and her eyes raised to his.

"But if I didn't see you out, I couldn't do this." He captured her chin and slowly lowered his face to hers, giving her plenty of time to stop him, but she didn't.

Her eyes darted to his mouth and she licked her lips, her pink tongue leaving a smidgeon of wetness on her lush lower lip. It was like she'd licked his dick. He couldn't delay any longer.

His hand wrapped around the back of her neck. "Open for me." His lips were so close to hers that he could feel the warmth from her breath.

She obeyed without hesitation, her mouth opening slightly. His hand tightened, adjusting her head for his kiss. She was lush and wet, her fingers grasping his shirt, holding onto him as if he were the only thing in her world. That was perfect because he was going to be her dom and that meant he was the only thing that mattered in her world. He tipped her head, deepening the kiss and she moaned. It was a soft little sound that made him want to fuck her until she repeated that noise over and over again.

The elevator dinged and he stepped back, her lips and body following him for a quick moment before she blinked and straightened. He grinned. The little rabbit was his.

"After you." He put his hand on the side of the door to keep it from closing.

She stepped into the garage, her face flushed and her legs a little unsteady. He followed behind her, taking her arm to steady her. She didn't object as he led her to his car and pulled out his keys.

"This isn't my car," she said.

"It's mine." He opened the door. "Get in."

"Why are we at your car?"

His little rabbit wasn't too bright. "To finish what we

started in that elevator."

She stared at him, confusion in her lovely hazel eyes. Her lips were red from his kisses and he couldn't resist tasting them again. He bent, capturing her mouth but this time he didn't coax he demanded. Her body stiffened and her lips were tight and closed. Obviously, she wasn't ready to surrender. So, it was back to persuasion.

"Open for me." He ran his tongue over her lower lip before nipping that succulent flesh. She gasped, giving him the access he desired. His tongue dove into her mouth, exploring and caressing. Her hands tangled in his hair and her body pressed flush against his. She was so soft and warm, her belly cradling his cock as her breasts smashed against his chest. He was going to fuck her right here if he didn't stop. Not that it'd be the first time someone had gone at it in the garage, but his little rabbit wasn't ready to put on a show.

He broke the kiss but kept her engulfed in his arms. "Get in the car."

"What?" Her hazy, passion filled eyes were on his mouth as if it had the answers to all her problems.

"Get in the car or I'm going to put you on the hood and fuck you." That should get her moving.

"No." She moved all right but it was away from him and his car. "I need to go home."

"You need to get in my car." He was losing patience with his little sub.

She shook her head, backing away.

"Maggie, you want this as much as I do. Don't deny it."

"I…" She clutched at her throat. "I'm sorry, but I can't." She turned and hurried away.

"Damnit." He closed and locked his car before striding after her.

CHAPTER 9: Maggie

Maggie thought about running but that'd be a bit too dramatic, wouldn't it? Terry had only kissed her. That's it. A simple kiss except there'd been nothing simple about it. His footsteps behind her made her reconsider her decision not to run.

"Maggie, wait."

She stopped. She shouldn't have, but her feet weren't listening to her. If she were honest, none of her body was. It wanted this man. He made her feel sexy and alive, feelings she hadn't had in years.

"Where do you think you're going?" He stepped in front of her.

"I have to go home." She stared up at him, her eyes darting to his lips. They were so firm and sensual and had tasted wonderful.

"Don't be afraid of this." He put his hands on her shoulders.

"I'm not." She was. She didn't know him. She shouldn't

want him, but everything was all jumbled in her head. He was a stranger. He'd saved her. He was blunt and harsh. Yet, he made her feel cared for and safe.

"Don't lie to me."

"I'm not. I have to go home."

"Are you sure?" He stepped closer to her.

The scent of his cologne was intoxicating.

"I think we should go to my place and...talk about our situation."

"What situation?" She'd thought he was going to be vulgar again and honestly, she was a little disappointed that he wanted to talk.

"This attraction"—his hands skimmed down her arms, making her blood sizzle—"and why you keep running from it."

"I told you. I don't have time—"

"For a relationship. I know, but it doesn't have to take too much time." He moved closer. "A few hours a couple of days a week or more if you'd like."

"Y-you want me to see you just for sex?" She'd never been that kind of girl. She'd married her college sweetheart, but that life was over. All she had to look forward to were days and days of celibacy while she raised her children alone. Being the kind of woman who met a man only for sex did have its appeal.

"For sex, yes, but not just." His lips were by her ear. "We'll talk and eat and...play games."

"Games? What kind of games?" She struggled not to lean into him.

He straightened, looking down at her and his grin made her toes curl. He wasn't talking about board games.

"Ones we'll both enjoy." He took her arm. "Come. We'll

discuss all of this at my place."

"I can't." She stepped back and he let go.

"No sex. Unless you want to." He took her hand. "Come, Maggie. You don't want to go home yet, do you? We'll have a drink and talk. I swear, I won't try anything"—he stared at her lips—"not even a kiss." His eyes sparkled with passion when they met hers. "You don't want to be alone again tonight."

It was like he was reading her mind. What would a few minutes or hour hurt? Nothing, except she couldn't afford to pay Tina, the babysitter, to stay longer than necessary. Plus, Tina had school tomorrow. It wasn't fair to keep her up late. "No. I can't tonight."

"Where's your car?" He smiled as he took her arm.

"This way."

He escorted her in the direction of her car. She should break the contact, but she liked touching him, leaning on him. He was so strong and confident. It made her feel safe and special.

"I'll pick you up tomorrow at seven. Wear a skirt." He looked her over, his eyes caressing. "Green, if you have one and a white blouse."

"What?" She'd never had a man tell her how to dress. She wanted to slap her forehead. That wasn't the most important part of his statement. "I can't go out with you tomorrow."

"Saturday then, but no later." He pulled her against him, engulfing her in his warmth. "I can't wait too long to have you."

The words were like liquid fire. Her husband had barely touched her in years. She deserved this, but it didn't matter. She was a mother, not a young woman without responsibilities. She needed to be with her kids, especially since the divorce. She placed her hands on his chest, memorizing the feel and then pushed away and started walking again. "I'm sorry but I can't. I told you—"

"You said you couldn't go home with me tonight, implying that you could and would another day." His tone was even but firm. He wasn't angry, just stating the facts.

"I did not."

"You did. You said, *No, I can't tonight.*"

She had said that. "I didn't mean that I could another night."

"That's what specifying tonight means."

She stopped in front of her car. "Terry, I appreciate this." She smiled sadly up at him. If only she'd met him at a different time. "You have no idea the gift you've given me by showing an interest, but I can't go out with you." She stood on her tiptoes and gave him a quick kiss on his cheek.

He stared past her, horror, disgust and shock waging war on his face.

"What's wrong? Are you okay?"

CHAPTER 10: Terry

"Is that your car?" Terry had never seen a bigger piece of junk. It was an old Ford something or other. It was covered in rust and had so many dents, he couldn't even tell the model any longer.

"I know it's not great but it gets me from here to there."

"I don't see how?" He walked around the car. "This thing isn't safe to be on the road."

"It is too." She crossed her arms over her chest.

"When was the last time it broke down?"

"What difference..."

He was in no mood for avoidance. He shot her a look.

"A week ago but that's why I know it's safe to drive. They fixed it."

"They should've put it out of its misery."

"I have to go." She pulled her keys from her purse.

Great. Now, he'd pissed her off. "I told you before I was brusque."

"Rude is more accurate."

"Yeah, probably." He grinned. Damn, she was a grumpy one. A good, hard fuck would put her in a better mood.

"Well, I don't like it. Good night." She got into the car.

He hurried to the driver's side and tapped the glass. She started the car and rolled down the window.

"When you change your mind, call me." He handed her his card.

"I won't change my mind." She tossed it on the passenger seat without looking at it.

That hurt. Usually, his profession impressed women enough to disregard his rudeness—that and the money he made. "Don't tell me you enjoy going home alone night after night." He bent so he could smell her perfume-vanilla and strawberries. She smelled like a dessert he was dying to eat. "Do you touch yourself when you're lying awake in your lonely bed?"

Her face turned bright red. "Goodnight." She tried to put up the window but he refused to move so she took her finger off the button.

"Maggie, you're a beautiful, sensuous woman with desires and needs. You deserve someone who can take care of you. Someone who'll make you come so hard you scream and then do it all over again."

The pulse at her neck was beating a cha-cha and her nipples were hard under her blouse. He reached inside the car, running his hand slowly down her shoulder toward her breast, giving her ample time to stop him. His cock throbbed, dancing to the beat in her throat. When she didn't move, his fingers skimmed over her breast. "Just listening to me makes you wet. Imagine how you'd feel when I kissed you"—he squeezed her nipple lightly, just enough to tease—"here."

"Goodnight." She shrugged his hand away and put the car in gear.

"Maggie..."

She began to drive away, forcing him to extricate himself from the window.

"Think about me tonight when you touch yourself. Dream about me and know it'll be a hundred times better when I'm really there."

CHAPTER 11: Maggie

"No, no. Don't do this. Hang on. You can make it. Only another few yards." Maggie wanted to cry or scream at the heavens. Her car could not die now. She was almost out of the parking lot of La Petite Mort Club. She stepped harder on the gas, causing the car to jump forward and shake. *Please, that can't be its death rattle. Not now. Not here.* Why were these things happening to her? She was a good person. She went to church, took care of her kids and was kind to everyone she met. She hit the steering wheel and pushed the gas pedal down all the way. "Get me home or down the street. Die anywhere but here."

As the car continued jerking through the parking lot, she kept bargaining with it. "If you make it around the corner, I'll take you to a car wash. I swear." She could not have her car die in the parking lot of the sex club. It'd be too embarrassing, especially if Terry saw her. The car shook, sputtering its last gasp. She dropped her head onto the steering wheel. This was what she got for taking the devil a container of cookies.

She stepped out of her car and looked at the building. No one was around. Maybe, she'd gotten lucky. She reached into her car and grabbed her phone as a black Mercedes pulled out of the garage. She knew that car. She'd ridden in that car.

That was not a spark of pleasure in her heart—or actually lower, much lower. She did not, could not be around that man any more or she'd do whatever he wanted. She took a deep breath, steadying her nerves. She'd send him along like she'd done earlier...when he'd had his hand on her breast. The tiny spark of desire was now a steady flame, throbbing between her legs. She had to get out of there or at least, have someone coming before he stopped. She turned on her phone, searching for the number for the tow truck.

CHAPTER 12: Terry

Terry watched Maggie drive away, her car sputtering and jerking. He grinned, unable to believe his luck. Even as stubborn as she was, his little rabbit would have to admit she needed his help. He got into his car. That piece of junk she was driving wouldn't make it far.

As he pulled out of the parking garage, he chuckled. His night was looking up. He drove over by her and got out of his car. "Need some help?"

"No." She was looking at her phone. "I'm calling a tow truck."

"Let me take care of it." He captured her hand, pressing the button to disconnect her call.

"What are you...I was next in line."

"I'll take care of this."

"I can't let you do that."

"Yes, you can." He stepped closer, letting his command and control ease her worries. "I want to help you."

"I'm not having sex with you."

"I wasn't asking." He pulled out his phone and pressed a button. "Hey Mattie, I need you to send a tow truck to the Club. No. Not mine. A"—he stared at the car—"a blue piece of shit. You can't miss it."

"Stop it." She tugged on his arm.

"Hold on." He glanced at her. "You really don't want me to take care of this for you?"

"No." She bit her lip.

"Mattie, I'll call you back. No. Don't send the truck yet." He hung up and looked down at her.

She wore out of style, ill-fitting clothes and drove a junk car. Money was tight and that was perfect because he had no problem spending money on his sub. However, she'd baked him cookies as a "thank you" for him saving her and taking her home. That meant she had pride. His dick began to harden. He loved a sub with pride. It was so fulfilling helping them learn to trust him with their dignity. The sex was always fantastic in these situations, but she wasn't ready to trust him with that gift yet.

"It won't cost anything. Mattie's a friend." He'd have to get Mattie on board. He wouldn't lie to her. That was never the right way to earn trust, but he could work out some scenario with his friend—a barter of services.

"Really? He'll tow the car for free?" She didn't seem to believe him. "That's some friend."

"I've helped him out in the past." That was true. He'd helped Mattie with some legal issues with the business, but he'd charged of course. He wouldn't the next time.

"You sure?"

He nodded.

"And he's a real mechanic?"

"Yes." He almost laughed. "He owns Mattie's Machines. It's a real shop and he's an excellent mechanic."

"Well…" She nibbled on her lip and he fought not to bend down and lick it. "Okay then."

"Good girl."

She bristled a bit but she'd get used to the endearment. He dialed Mattie. "Yeah, come for the car and let me know what it'll take to fix it."

"I'm paying for that," she said.

Oh, she'd pay for all of it, but not with money. He nodded at her. "No, the keys will be in it. I don't want to hear that you can't pick up an abandoned car. Hold on." He held the phone out and snapped a picture of her vehicle and another one of her plate. He pressed a few buttons. "I texted you the pictures. Now, you know what car it is." He laughed. "I told you it was a piece of shit."

"Hey."

He ignored her. "Yeah, call me. Tomorrow is fine." He hung up the phone and put it in his pocket. He walked to the other side of his car and opened the door. "Maggie." It was a command and she really didn't have many options.

"You're taking me to my house, right?"

Oh, his little rabbit had a lot to learn. "I'll take you wherever you want to go."

"Home. I want to go home."

"Are you sure? You sound like you're convincing yourself."

"I'm not. I mean, I am sure. I have to go home."

Have to, not want to. That was an improvement. "Then, I'll take you home." He'd rather their first time be at his place but hers would do. Right now, he'd probably agree to a fast fuck in the car. He'd been spoiled by the Club. Everyone in the place was looking for sex. Yes, there were often negotiations and sometimes it took several days, but the outcome was never in question. With Maggie, he wasn't one hundred percent sure they were going to have sex, tonight or ever. He was ninety-nine percent sure, but not one hundred and that one percent of uncertainty was killing him.

"Th-thank you." She got into the car and he shut the door.

Tonight, his little rabbit would be his. He walked to the driver's side and got in, glancing at her. "Relax."

He reached across the car and took her hand. Hers was so small compared to his. He hadn't wanted to protect or take care of a woman like this in years.

CHAPTER 13: Maggie

Maggie should slip her hand from Terry's warm grasp, but she didn't. She liked having a man in her life, someone to help her, someone she could lean on. A lot of women didn't mind being alone but that wasn't her. She used to wish she could be like that, but if nothing else, her divorce taught her that wishing didn't change anything.

"Don't be afraid of me. Of this. I'll never hurt you. You know that, right?"

"I-I do." She lied. He wouldn't rape her or hit her, but he would hurt her. This would just be sex for him and she needed more than that. Like she knew she wasn't good alone, she also knew she wasn't the kind of woman who had casual sex with strange men.

"There's no reason to be afraid of this." He stopped the car at a stop light and moved his hand to cup her cheek. "We should relish it. Attraction like this doesn't happen often. It's a gift."

She wanted to lean into his touch but instead, shifted her

head away. "Attraction like this is a curse not a gift."

He frowned as he put his hand on the wheel and started driving again. "A curse? No. Absolutely, not."

"Yes, it is because we can't do anything about it."

"We most certainly can."

"Fine, then we won't."

"We will."

His tone was authoritative and she was getting a little sick of it. "No. We won't. I won't. I don't have flings and that's what this would be." If it weren't for the kids, she might consider it, but she didn't have time.

"It won't be a fling. Nothing so insubstantial."

"Please. This isn't leading to marriage."

"God no. I'll never marry again."

"Me either." Instinctively, she crossed her arms over her chest to protect herself—her heart. It was silly to be hurt by his words, but a tiny part of her—the part that, apparently, hadn't learned not to hope—had wanted him to say that he didn't know where it would lead. It might've given her the excuse to surrender to his commands and her desire, but Terry was honest to a fault.

"So, you never plan on having sex again?" He glanced at her, a spark of challenge in his eyes.

"What? I never said that."

"You did. You said that you didn't have flings and the only other option you seem to be able to see is marriage. Then, you said you won't marry again. Ergo, no more sex. Ever." He turned down her road.

"Well..." God, he was right. She liked sex. She didn't want to imagine never having it again.

He pulled over and stopped the car, taking off his seatbelt and capturing her chin, forcing her to look at him. "Maggie, I want you. We can make this work." He kissed her softly. "You don't really want to go without sex, do you?" His tongue trailed across her lips.

She opened for his kiss, unable to stop herself. There was something about him—his roughness, his honesty that drew her.

He held her still for his kisses while his other hand skimmed over her breasts. "You were made for sex. All these curves and lushness." He kissed down her neck. "I want to bury my face in your pussy and worship you."

Heaven help her, even his foul language made her heart pound. David had never spoken to her like this. She should be offended but instead, the throbbing between her legs increased—chanting, "yes, yes."

His hand trailed between her thighs. She wanted to relax, to open for him. She wanted sex. Why shouldn't she get to have sex? Her ex already had a new wife. Her legs drifted open.

"Good girl." His lips captured hers as his large hand cupped her pussy.

She moaned against his mouth. The pressure, the touch felt so good. Lord help her, she wanted this man.

He removed his hand from between her legs and unhooked her seatbelt, pulling her into his arms. She opened wider, melting against him and he deepened the kiss, his tongue tangling with hers. He grabbed her head with one hand, keeping her still for his invasion as the other cupped her ass, squeezing.

She tightened her arms, which had somehow gotten wrapped around his neck. She needed to be closer to him. He nipped her lip and she moaned, feeling it all the way to the ache between her legs. He knew too because his hand slid under her ass, moving closer to the place that begged to be touched.

Lights splashed over them as another car drove slowly past before disappearing down the road.

"Fuck." Terry squeezed her ass once more as he broke the kiss.

"What?" She blinked, her mind filled with nothing but lust. "Oh." She untangled her arms, glad for the darkness because her face had to be as red as a tomato. She'd almost had sex in a car. On the street. Where anyone could see them. Her head dropped back against the seat.

"Fuck." He repeated as he started the car and pulled onto the road.

She closed her eyes. This was so embarrassing. They were in her neighborhood. If anyone had seen her...

He turned into a driveway and stopped the car. He leaned over and kissed her hard. That was all it took, one touch of his lips, and she couldn't think of anything but the feelings he was stirring inside her—desire, passion. Things she hadn't felt in too long. His fingers skimmed across her pubic mound, light and fleeting. She wiggled and he deepened the kiss and the pressure, one long finger sliding between her legs, over and over.

"We should go inside or at least put my car in your garage." His breath whispered over her lips.

"M-my garage?" Her heart stalled. They were at her house. In her driveway. Tina could be looking out the window. "Oh god." She pushed at his hand that was still wedged between her legs. "I've got to go." She threw open the door and hurried to the house as she fumbled in her purse for her keys.

The car door slammed and a few moments later Terry was behind her.

"Maggie, don't run away from me. Let's talk inside."

She almost laughed but it was too sad. This was it. The exact time that this, whatever it was, would end. She took a shaky breath. She'd always have her memories of this rich, sexy man wanting her.

CHAPTER 14: Terry

Terry stared down at Maggie, his heart beating an erratic rhythm. If she turned him away now, after she'd been so giving and responsive in the car, he might weep. He hadn't wanted a woman like this in a long time. "Let me come inside." His dick hardened even more at the double entendre. He cleared his throat. "We can just talk, if you want." She was as hot for him as he was for her. If they were in a house alone, they'd do a lot more than talk and they both knew it.

"I don't think you want to come inside." There was a sad smile on her lips—lips that were swollen and red from his kisses.

"Oh, I absolutely do want to *come* inside." Her mouth, her pussy, her ass. Everywhere she'd let him.

Her eyes widened and her face heated as she realized what she'd said.

"And I guarantee we'll both like that." He brushed a strand of hair from her cheek. It was soft. She was soft and he was excruciatingly hard.

"Okay. I'll make some coffee." She put her key in the lock and opened the door, stepping inside.

Yes, yes, and yes. They were finally going to fuck. He'd move slowly with the dominance. She was such a natural sub. It wouldn't take long for her to discover the pleasure they both would have with her submission. Something moved on the couch. No, not something. Someone. A young girl. Teenager but she was lumpy, holding something to her chest.

"Shhh. I just got him to sleep." The girl stared at the pile of blankets in her arms.

Terry's erection fled and his heart stopped. It wasn't blankets. It was a child.

Maggie strode over to the young girl, taking the baby from her arms. "Did he give you too much trouble?"

"Not really. He was a little fussy." The babysitter's eyes darted to Terry. "He woke and wanted you. I know you're trying to get him off the bottle, but he was so fussy. I gave him one and held him until he went back to sleep."

"That's fine, Tina."

Maggie had a kid. He should've expected it. She was of that age and she was the type—giving, motherly.

"The other two?" asked Maggie.

"They were great," said the babysitter.

"Three kids? You have three kids." This was not at all what he'd expected.

The house was a disaster with packing boxes all over and kids' toys and clothes. The mess didn't bother him. They'd stay at his place but...the kids. Three. Three! And one was a baby, around two years old.

"Yes." Maggie turned toward him, a gleam in her eyes. "Did

you still want that coffee?"

"What? No. I mean, I really should be going." His feet moved backward as he spoke. He wasn't getting involved with a woman who had children. No way. No how. He'd raised his kids.

"I didn't think so." She smiled but it didn't reach her eyes. "Goodnight, Terry and thank you for everything."

He hurried out the door and to his car. That was a narrow escape. It was too bad he hadn't fucked her at the Club or in the car. He still wanted her but didn't need the hassle.

CHAPTER 15: Terry

Terry sat in Ethan's office drinking and playing cards—pastimes he usually enjoyed but not tonight. Nope, his night had tanked as soon as he'd walked into Maggie's house.

"These are fucking fantastic." Ethan ate another cookie.

Terry grunted and stood. It wasn't Maggie's cookies he wanted to eat but the rest of her was off limits. He hadn't been denied something he'd wanted in years. He'd forgotten how much it sucked.

"Going into the Club?" Ethan picked up the cards.

"Nah. Home."

"It's early." Ethan's blue eyes studied him. "What's wrong with you? I didn't expect to see you again tonight after leaving with Maggie."

"Tired." He was more than tired. He was in a crappy mood. He had been since he'd found out about Maggie's kids.

There was a knock on the door.

"Ethan," hollered Nick.

"Back here," yelled Ethan.

"My timing is excellent," mumbled Terry as Nick and his fiancé, Sarah, walked in.

"Hey," said Ethan, smiling at Sarah. "What brings you two here?"

"We're going to explore the Club for a bit." Nick gave Terry a curt nod, pulling Sarah a little closer to his side.

Terry's nagging about a prenuptial agreement had put a wedge between him and Nick. He should be happy for his friend. He would be except he knew how bad marriages got when they ended and most of them did end. So, he'd continue harassing the fool until Nick either agreed to sign a prenup or got married. Nick was worth a lot of money and he needed to think with the head on his shoulders, not the one between his legs.

"Have fun." Ethan grinned at the couple as he stuffed another cookie in his mouth.

"Well, I'm out of here." He'd been irritable before and having these two around wouldn't make it better.

"Cookies?" Nick moved forward.

Terry thought a moment about being an ass and saying they were his but he was too tired. Usually, he enjoyed arguing. He was a lawyer, but tonight he wasn't in the mood.

"They're Terry's," teased Ethan.

Nick grabbed two cholate chips cookies and turned to Sarah. "What kind do you want?"

"None for me." She eyed Terry nervously.

He hadn't been overly friendly with her the few times they'd met. He should be. If he ostracized Sarah, Nick would never speak with him again, let alone listen to him. "Try some. They're very good." He snatched the container from beneath

Nick's hands and held it out to her. "Please, have one."

"They're fabulous." Ethan tipped his chair, so he could grab a few more.

"Thank you." Sarah looked Terry in the eyes and he almost understood what made all these guys—Ethan, Nick and even Hunter—want to protect her.

She looked innocent, untarnished by the world, but he'd talked to her in the Viewing when she'd first come to the Club and she was stronger than she appeared.

"These are great." Nick stuffed the second cookie in his mouth and grabbed two more.

Sarah took a bite of hers and almost moaned. "They're delicious. Did you make them?"

Ethan burst out laughing and Nick almost choked on his cookie.

"Terry? Terry can't cook," muttered Nick.

"I could. I just don't want to." He probably could if he tried, but he never did. He was busy and he hated being home alone. Beast, the dog he'd adopted from Nick, helped but his house was still lonely.

"Right." Nick grabbed another cookie and handed it to Sarah.

"Who made them?" Sarah finished her first one and took the other from Nick.

"A friend of Terry's." Ethan emphasized friend.

"I smell a story." Nick grabbed Sarah's hand and pulled her down on the couch next to him. "Spill."

"Do you want me to tell it?" Ethan leaned his elbows on the table, grinning at Terry.

"There's nothing to tell." Terry sighed and sat down. "But if

I don't explain, Ethan will blow this all out of proportion and Nick will never stop his incessant teasing."

"Me?" Nick touched his chest. "You're the asshole of the group not me."

"Honey, you can be an asshole too." Sarah kissed his cheek to take the sting from her words.

Ethan laughed and Terry decided that he might have to give this woman another chance once Nick signed the prenup.

"True, but I'm working on it." Nick kissed her hand.

"Jesus." He sent Ethan a disgusted look. "Why do you even let him and Patrick in here? Are you trying to make me vomit?"

"Jealous," said Nick.

"Hardly. I did my time." His marriage hadn't ended well. Shit, who was he kidding? Most of his married life had been tense and unsatisfying.

"Back to the story of the cookies," said Ethan, keeping the peace as usual.

"Fine." Terry stretched out his legs and settled against the seat. "Ethan's last party had some issues."

"Don't they always when you let in non-members," said Nick. It wasn't a question.

"Yeah, but this was worse than usual." Ethan glanced at Terry. "A woman was almost raped."

"Jesus." Nick squeezed Sarah's hand.

"What happened?" asked Sarah. "Is she okay?"

"Thanks to her hero." Ethan smirked as he turned toward Terry, batting his lashes.

"Terry?" Nick laughed. "He's the last guy I'd see in that role."

"Hey!" He may be brusque but he'd never let someone get

74

raped.

"I didn't mean you'd hurt a woman. I know you wouldn't do that, but I didn't expect you to…What exactly did you do?" asked Nick.

"I happened to see a woman who definitely didn't belong here. She was heading toward the playrooms, so I followed her. She went into a room and there were several guys—"

"Several?" Sarah's face paled. "That poor woman must've been terrified.

"Renee was in there and the—"

"Renee likes to get fucked by numerous men at once," Nick explained to Sarah.

"Really?" She made a face that said it was clearly not her thing.

"Glad you're not into that because that's never going to happen." Nick's hand rested on her thigh. "You're mine and only mine."

"Please you two," said Ethan. "I just ate. Go into the Club if you want to act like that."

"Soon." Nick's hand caressed her leg but he faced Terry. "So, go on. What did you do to deserve a hero's cape?"

"The guys weren't members and they didn't understand the scene and the rules," said Terry.

"That's not an excuse and you know it. Everyone is told the rules when they enter," said Ethan. "No forced anything. Ever."

"I know but you also know that people come here for these events with preconceived ideas about sex clubs and they're usually wrong."

"And that's why I tell them." A muscle ticked in Ethan's jaw. Consent was the number one rule around here.

"Anyway, they weren't going to let Maggie leave so I stepped in."

"Was there a fight?" Nick looked at Ethan. "Where were the bouncers?"

"Nearby, just not in the room," said Terry. "And no, there wasn't a fight. I got Maggie out and then texted Ethan."

"That was so brave of you." Sarah smiled at him.

He shrugged. "Anyone would've done it. Any member anyway. That kind of stuff doesn't go on here."

"Absolutely, and those guys will never be back. I'm even reviewing the members who invited them," said Ethan. "I don't need that shit around here."

"So, where did these cookies come from." Nick took Sarah's hand and ate the last bite of her cookie.

"Maggie baked them for Terry as a thank you," said Ethan.

"That was nice of her," said Sarah.

Nick looked from one guy to another. "Wait a minute."

Terry almost groaned. Nick was like a terrier ferreting out information. "What?"

"Why were you following this woman?"

"I told you. She obviously didn't belong here." He smirked. "You should've seen her looking around the main part of the Club. She was bumping into everyone, her eyes huge. She'd never seen anything like this place."

"Then why did she go to the playrooms?" asked Nick. "There's a sign and it's pretty damn clear that it isn't the bathrooms down there."

"She was looking for a friend," said Ethan. "Vicky Givens."

"She's a friend of Vicky Givens?" Nick snorted. "She can't be innocent."

"Not exactly a friend," said Terry. "She was Vicky's sister-in-law before she got divorced. She thought they were still friends"

"It had to be some kind of mean joke on Vicky's part," said Ethan. "You know the bitch does that crap."

"Oh, that poor woman," said Sarah. "She must've been so hurt."

"She was. She cried most of the way home," said Terry. Except when he'd gotten her to think about sex.

"You took her home?" Nick's lips twitched.

"Yeah. So? I didn't want her calling an Uber after what she'd gone through."

Ethan cleared his throat.

"There's more to this story," prodded Nick.

"No. There's not." He wanted to leave but then he'd never, ever hear the end of this.

"Terry likes her," mumbled Ethan behind his hand.

"I don't. Yes, I was attracted to her but that's all."

"Is she really that innocent?" asked Nick. "That's not your type."

Terry shrugged. "You know me. Everywhere else I follow my head but here I follow my dick."

Sarah's eyes dropped to her lap.

"Please. Nick's said worse, I'm sure." He didn't need this fake innocent crap.

"Yes, but"—she smiled, eyes gleaming with mischief as her gaze met his—"you should get that printed on a T-shirt."

"Maybe, I will." He laughed.

"So, why the cookies and not a few nights of fucking?" asked Nick.

"I was angling for that, but she has kids." Terry's shoulders

Ellis O. Day

sagged, suddenly tired again.

"Three," said Ethan.

"So," said Nick.

"I don't want a relationship and women with children, especially with young kids, don't want to just fuck."

"Did you ask her," asked Sarah.

"I offered."

"Oh." Sarah's eyes widened.

"I told you, Terry's crass," said Nick.

"But I'm honest. It's best."

"Yeah. I guess." Sarah glanced at the container of cookies. "They really are good. Do you have her name or phone number?"

"Why? You going to ask her to bake you some?" Terry didn't want any of them around Maggie. The way Maggie had eyed Ethan she might take him up on an offer to become less innocent and if anyone were going to teach her the fun that could be had between two consenting adults, it was him.

"Annie's looking for a pastry chef."

"That's right. She is," said Nick.

"I don't have her phone number." He didn't need Maggie hanging around Annie. Annie, Patrick's girlfriend, was a perpetual busybody, always trying to arrange everyone's life into what she thought was best.

"How are you going to return her container?" asked Sarah.

He looked at the plastic dish. "I wasn't."

"You have to," said Sarah.

"She didn't say she wanted it back."

"It's understood. If you give someone food or take it to a party—unless the container is a throw away—it's returned to

78

the owner." Sarah looked at all of them like they were idiots.

"There's a rule about this shit?" He looked at the guys and they both shrugged.

"You can ask Annie if you don't believe me." Sarah almost huffed.

"No. I'm sure you're right." He had no idea about this kind of crap.

"You can give it to Mattie," said Ethan, lips twitching.

"What's my brother have to do with this?" asked Nick.

"Maggie's car broke down in the parking lot and"—Ethan wiped his eyes, trying not to laugh—"Terry saved her again."

"A regular knight in shining armor," joked Nick.

"It was before I knew she had kids. My motives were hardly chivalrous."

"You know what? Give it to me." Ethan held out his hand. "I'll take it to her. She's going to need a ride to Mattie's when her car is fixed. I'll be more than happy to give her a *ride*."

Terry was going to punch him in the mouth if he kept emphasizing ride like that. "I'll take care of it." Ethan wasn't getting near her, but his friend was right. She was going to need someone to drive her to Mattie's garage.

"You should give it to Ethan," said Nick with laughter in his dark eyes. "A lonely, divorcee could use something to brighten her day."

"Exactly," said Ethan.

"She has three kids, remember?" He almost growled.

"Yeah, but Sarah is right. She may be up for a little pleasure for herself off and on." Ethan's blue eyes heated. "Couldn't blame her and I do know how to make a woman feel good."

"Fuck you." He stood, grabbing the container. "If anyone's

79

going to give her pleasure, it's going to be me." For some reason he wasn't tired anymore.

"Hey, there are still cookies in there," said Ethan.

Terry turned the container upside down, spilling cookies and crumbs all over the table.

"Fuck. You didn't need to do that." Ethan stared at the mess. "Asshole."

He smirked as he strode to the door. Ethan hated disorder almost as much as Terry hated someone encroaching on his territory. Maggie was his. Now, he just had to convince her of that.

CHAPTER 16: Terry

Terry pulled into the driveway at Maggie's house. He grabbed the container from the car and strode to the front door.

Maggie opened it before he could knock. She had her phone in her hand. "Yes, he's here now."

"Who are you talking to?" He handed her the container.

She took it, dropping it behind her on a table by the door, before holding up her finger and signaling him to wait. One day he'd give her a spanking for acting like that.

"Thanks, but I can take an Uber to the garage." Her eyes met his and she flushed a pretty pink.

Damn, he wanted this woman and he wasn't going to have her, not tonight anyway. Not with a house full of kids.

"Goodbye, Ethan." She hung up the phone, slipping it into her pocket.

"You called Ethan? How'd you get his number?" He was going to murder his friend.

"I called the Club. I—"

"Why would you call the Club?" He tried to keep his tone neutral but she'd called Ethan. The man who had every woman licking the palm of his...whatever he wanted her to lick.

"Because you didn't tell me where you had my car towed. It must've slipped your mind as you raced out the door." She crossed her arms over her chest.

"I didn't run out the door." He might have. Those few moments were a bit of a blur.

She raised her brow.

"I may have overreacted a bit." That was as much of a concession as he was willing to give. "But you could've warned...told me you had three kids." His voice lowered on the last two words.

"There's no reason to whisper like it's a dirty little secret."

"I didn't." He kind of had, but not intentionally.

Up went her brow again.

He moved a step closer. "Look. I don't want this to be the end."

Her shoulders slumped and she sighed. "I'm sorry, but—"

"I know you can't tonight but this weekend, we can..." He hesitated. Usually, he'd be blunt and say they'd fuck, but he wasn't stupid. She didn't like it when he cursed. He'd teach her to like it but until then, he'd curb his language. "Go out." *And fuck.*

"I-I can't." Her hand fluttered as if she were going to touch his arm and then it dropped to her side. "I have to work—"

"Great. I'll pick you up."

"My car should be done by then, won't it?"

He shrugged. "Maybe." It should be. Mattie was a very good mechanic.

"Where is my car?"

"Mattie's Machines."

"Oh, you did mention that. What's the number?" She pulled her phone from her pocket.

"Why? I'll take you there when the car is done."

"I need to call them and tell them my contact information."

He wanted to argue that he'd take care of it, of her, of everything, but there was a stubborn tilt to her chin that he recognized. It was universal to all women. It signaled that this was getting into dangerous, irrational territory. He pulled out his phone, found Mattie's work number and showed it to her.

"Thank you." She put it into her phone and then dialed.

"He's closed." Not that it mattered because Mattie would call him no matter what she said.

"Oh." She hung up, slipping her phone back into her pocket. "I'll call in the morning."

"Fine." He counted to five, reminding himself that he was glad she was being so stubborn. It'd make her submission so much sweeter. "Let's talk about this weekend."

"Terry, I can't."

"Okay. Then during the week. How about Tuesday? I'll pick you up. We can go out for dinner. A movie. Dancing. You pick." As long as they ended up at his place afterwards, they could go anywhere she wanted.

"I can't. I'm sorry." She stood on tiptoe and kissed his cheek. "I like you. I do, but I truly don't have time to see anyone." She started to shut the door but hesitated. "Thank you for...for everything. You're a very nice man."

"Don't ever call me that." Oh, he was so not a nice man.

"What? A nice guy?"

He cringed. Nice guys did not get laid.

"Like it or not, that's what you are." She tried unsuccessfully not to smile.

He leaned down so his lips were by her ear. "Give me one night and I'll have you thinking a lot of things about me and not one of them will be that I'm nice."

"Oh? What will they be?" She didn't move away.

He'd take that as a good sign. "Hmm." He let his lips caress her ear. "Insatiable. Fantastic. The best you ever had." He smiled, letting her feel his grin against her cheek. "Huge."

She laughed as she took a step back, but there was unease in the sound, as if she were nervous. "Tempting, but I can't."

He followed her. "I can make you forget about everything. All your worries. All your fears. Give me one night."

"I can't." She pushed on his chest and he backed up.

"You can." He took her hand. "You deserve some time for you." Her skin was soft and warm. She smelled like vanilla. He wondered if she tasted as good.

"I-I don't have time. I'm sorry."

"Make time." He took her face in his hands and slowly leaned in, giving her plenty of time to stop him, but she didn't. He captured her lips in a soft caress, banking his passions. Now, was about persuading not conquering. He broke the kiss but stayed close enough that he could feel her breath on his lips. "You're a beautiful woman with needs and desires. You're not just a mother."

"I have too much to do." She took a step into the house. "I have three kids to care for and a job. Plus, I have to pack up the house." She took a deep, shaky breath. "We didn't meet at the right time." She took another step. "Goodnight and thank you

84

again." She closed the door.

Terry stood there, not sure what to do. This had never happened to him before, not even when he'd been a gangly teenager. She'd shut the door in his face. Refused him. Well, she'd have to see him again when he drove her to the garage to get her car. He turned, pulling his phone from his pocket and dialing Mattie's personal number.

CHAPTER 17: Terry

Terry circled a line on the itemized asset list before handing it to Dan, one of the newer lawyers at the firm. "Talk to our client about this, but first do some digging."

"Digging? On what? That's one of their six houses." Dan stared at the paper.

"Yes, but look at what they're stating the value is." He watched the younger man. He was willing to teach but the student needed some instincts.

"It's lower than the other properties but it says here that Mr. White's parents live there." Dan looked up at him, as if that explained everything.

"And he, therefore, wants to keep it in the divorce." Terry tapped his pen on the desk.

"Well, yeah. Mrs. White's not contesting that."

"But we should."

"Terry." Dan sounded disgusted. "His parents live there."

"Really? Do you know this for a fact?"

"No, but he wouldn't lie about—"

"During a divorce, everyone lies about everything."

"I don't know."

"I do." He'd learned that from his own divorce. Morgan, his ex, had lied constantly and had taken everything they'd built—their house, their cars, his firm and his kids. He'd had to start all over. "Does Mr. White seem like the type of man to put his parents in a less than stellar home?"

"Ah…no. Actually, he doesn't."

"So, either they don't live there or that property is worth more than he's stating." His cell phone rang. It was Mattie. "Go. Dig into every one of those assets."

"Got it." Dan grabbed the files and left.

Terry answered his phone. "Hey Mattie, is the car ready?" He couldn't wait to see Maggie again and press his case.

"Ready? No. I've seen pieces of junk before but this…It ain't worth fixing," said Mattie.

"You sure?" That was even better, but Maggie wasn't going to be happy. His little rabbit liked her independence.

"Yeah. Whoever fixed it the last time did a shit-fuck job. They might as well have taped the parts together. You want me to call the lady who owns the car and give her the bad news?"

"I'll take care of it and send me the bill, not her."

"Got it. Hey, what do you want me to do with the car?"

"Junk it." Terry hung up the phone. This was perfect. He could help her again. He'd prove to her that she could trust him with everything—her life, her body, her pleasure.

He pushed the contact button for Maggie. It rang and rang. Damn, she needed to learn to answer when he called. If only they were at the point where he could punish her for this. His dick perked up at the thought of her begging him for release.

Her voice mail picked up. "Maggie, it's Terry." Soon he wouldn't have to announce who he was. She'd know his voice. "Mattie called about your car. It can't be repaired."

His intercom buzzed.

"Your three o'clock is here," said Ms. Richards, his assistant.

"Call me when you get this." He hung up before pressing the button for the intercom. "Send him in."

CHAPTER 18: Maggie

Maggie wanted to fling her phone across the room. This couldn't be happening. It couldn't. She dialed Terry's number but it went directly to voice mail. She didn't bother to leave a message. There was nothing he could do. She needed her car. She couldn't afford another one but she was going to have to find the money somewhere.

She could ask David for a loan when he came to pick up the kids for the weekend. Of course, then she'd have to listen to him lecture her about budgets and spending. He didn't understand that she couldn't overspend. She didn't make enough to overspend. She barely made enough to keep the kids fed and clothed.

She had to find another way. Maybe, Terry's friend was wrong. She should've insisted that her car be towed to Tires and More but the thought of free towing had fuzzied her brain. She grabbed her phone and searched for Mattie's Machines. She called the number and a man answered.

"Hi, my car was towed there last night. It's a blue Ford

Focus. Sure, I'll wait." She paced and prayed that there'd been a mistake.

"Hi, this is Mattie," said a different man.

"Hi, my car was towed to your shop last night."

"Yeah. I thought Terry was going to call you."

"He did but isn't there something you can do to make it drivable? I don't need a promise of forever just make it work for now."

"I'm sorry, but it'd be a huge waste of money."

"I see. Okay." Maybe the mechanics at Tires and More could fix it for her. They'd done it before. Sure, it'd only lasted a week or so, but maybe this time... "I'll send a tow truck to get it."

"You don't have to do that. I have a call out to junk it. Bring me your title and I'll give you the money for the scrap."

"You were going to scrap it?" This was unbelievable. He had no right.

"Ah...yeah. Is that a problem?"

"Yes, that's a problem. You hadn't even talked to me."

"But Terry said—"

"Terry doesn't own the car. I do."

"Okay, miss, take it easy. The car is still here."

"It'd better be."

"It is."

"I'll be there to pay you and with a tow truck in"—she glanced at the time on her phone—"an hour."

"You don't owe—"

"You looked the car over, didn't you?" She should let him not charge her because of his friendship with Terry but right now, her pride had control of her brain.

"Yeah, but Terry—"

"It's my car. My bill. I'm paying for it." Luckily, she still had some room on one of her credit cards.

"Yes, ma'am." There was humor in his tone and if she were in front of him, she just might slap his face.

"Goodbye." She was so sick of men—all of them.

CHAPTER 19: Maggie

"You sure you can't wait?" Maggie asked the Uber driver.

"Nope. Sorry."

"Okay." Maggie handed him the money and got out of the car in the parking lot of Mattie's Machines. She hadn't thought it was possible but her day had gone downhill after her phone call with Mattie earlier.

David had shown up with his new wife and a surprise for the kids. He was taking them away for the weekend. She could barely afford macaroni and cheese and David was carting them to the amusement park. It wasn't fair.

On top of that, because of her stupid car, she'd had to call off work—again. Her boss had warned her that one more time and she was out of a job. She couldn't rely on her car. So, instead of packing, she'd spend tonight looking for a new job.

She inhaled deeply, fighting tears as she headed for the door. This was not Terry's fault. She was an adult. She'd agreed to let her car be towed here instead of to Tires and More which had been a bad decision. Not only could Terry's friend not fix her car, but since another mechanic had played around under the hood, Tires and More may not cover the repairs. Still, there was no going back in life, only forward. She opened the door and stepped inside. The building was clean but smelled of grease and oil—car smells, reminding her of her father.

He'd always been tinkering with their car—able to fix things himself instead of paying someone else to do it. She should've paid more attention instead of playing nearby, but she'd never been a tomboy type of girl. She'd loved her dresses and dolls.

A very attractive man came out of the garage area. He had black hair and brilliant blue eyes. He smiled at her and she almost melted onto the floor.

"Hello, can I help you with something?" He moved behind the counter.

"I'm Maggie. I spoke with—"

"Terry's friend." His smile grew wider and his eyes did a quick dart down her frame.

She should be offended but she wasn't. There was a look of appreciation in his gaze and he was damn fine looking. "Yeah, I guess you could call it that." She wouldn't. Terry didn't want to be friends. He wanted to be lovers. The sad thing was that he was the closest thing to a friend she had.

"I need to tell you, that you don't want to have the car towed anywhere else. Junk it."

That was easy for him to say. He probably had dozens of cars. "I appreciate your opinion and I'm sure you're a great mechanic, but I really need a car and whatever's wrong with it may be covered by their warrantee." She prayed it was because otherwise she had no idea how she was going to pay.

93

"I doubt that. Whoever fixed it the last time ripped you off." His eyes narrowed. "Mechanics like that should be fired or arrested."

"No. You can't be right." When it'd broken down again, she'd wondered about that. She hated mechanics. She knew nothing about cars and so many of them seemed to thrive on duping women.

"I'm really sorry, but I'm not wrong about your car."

"I-I think, I'll have them look at it anyway." She opened her purse. "What do I owe you?" She was trying hard not to cry. She couldn't afford to pay him, a tow truck and Tires and More. She could barely afford the Ubers she was going to have to take home and to work tomorrow.

"Why don't you come with me?" He came around the counter and went to take her arm but stopped, looking at his hands which were filthy. "Come sit down." He took a step toward the back room.

She stared at him but saw nothing, her mind whirling with worries. She was going to lose everything. "Can you make it drivable for a little while? Please."

"I'm sorry, but it wouldn't be safe. You could break down at any time." He stepped aside, gesturing for her to proceed him. "Please, have a seat and I'll get you some water."

She walked to the waiting room and sat. She had no idea what she was going to do.

"I'll be right back." He left.

A moment later a petite, red-headed, young woman, who was as filthy as a mechanic, stepped out of the garage area. "Mattie said to give you this." She handed Maggie a bottle of water.

94

"Thank you." She took it, staring at it. She wasn't thirsty. She was desperate.

"Are you okay?"

She nodded but a tear slipped down her cheek.

"Hey, don't cry. Mattie can fix anything." The woman sat next to her. "And he'll set up a payment plan for you, if that's the problem."

"Really?" There was hope.

"Yeah." The girl smiled. "Mattie's a great mechanic. He's taught me a lot."

"You're a mechanic?"

"Yeah." The younger woman blushed. "I've always loved cars. Learned about them from my dad."

"I used to watch my father. Actually, I'd sit and play with my dolls while he worked. I wish I'd paid attention."

"I love the work but..." The younger woman glanced down at her clothes and shrugged.

"The dirt washes off and the pay has to be better than being a hostess at Outback."

"I guess so, but at least you get to look like a woman."

"Honey." She took the younger girl's filthy hand. "Any male with eyes can see that you're a woman." The girl was gorgeous—petite but with a nice bosom and brilliant blue eyes that complemented her dark red hair.

Mattie came out of a back office. "Thanks, Leena." He barely looked at her.

"Sure, Mattie. Anytime." The young woman smiled at him and Maggie's heart broke for her. Leena was in love with Mattie and the man didn't even see her.

"Sorry, I was gone so long. My mom called." Mattie smiled

sheepishly as he sat down in the chair that Leena had vacated. "I couldn't brush her off, you know?"

"Absolutely." He was even more adorable now that she knew he respected his mother.

"Anyway, I called Terry and—"

"Why did you do that?" Okay, not quite as adorable as before.

"Ah…you were upset and I thought—"

"I can make my own decisions about my car."

"Of course, but—"

"Tell me what I owe you so I can leave." She stood.

"I can't do that."

"Why not?"

"Terry said—"

"I don't care what Terry said."

"You'd better," said Terry as he strode into the room.

CHAPTER 20: Terry

Terry was going to paddle a certain woman's ass if she didn't stop being so obstinate. It wasn't a side of her he liked.

Maggie's eyes widened for a moment and then her cheeks flushed with anger. Okay, maybe he'd enjoy this side of her. He did love to punish a disobedient sub.

"Thank you for your help, but I'm taking my car to Tires and More."

"So, you can get ripped off again?" He crossed his arms over his chest.

"That's my decision not yours." She was losing some of her steam.

"I told you, I'd take care of everything." He moved closer and his little rabbit froze, sensing the predator approaching. "You need to trust me. I'll take care of this...of you."

"I don't need you to take care of me." She stepped forward and poked his chest. "I don't need any man to take care of me. I won't allow any man to take care of me ever again."

His control was legendary, but he hadn't gone this long

without sex since college. "Soon, you'll beg me to take care of you."

"I will never." She turned and stormed out the door.

"How did she get here?" Terry glanced at Mattie.

"Uber and she let him leave."

Good. That meant he had time. He'd let her stew for a few minutes and then go to her. She paced in the parking lot, her stride quick and her back stiff. He'd never realized rabbits had tempers.

"I'm surprised," said Mattie.

"About what?" She was glorious in her fury, her hair a riotous mess of curls—when loose they'd cascade down her back or over her breasts with just her nipples peeking out.

"I've only seen you with those CEO, model-thin types."

He shrugged. He had no reason to explain himself. His cock was his compass and Maggie was due north.

"If you're not interested, I love a woman with curves in all the right places. She certainly has that." Mattie inhaled. "A man could lose himself inside her for days—so ripe and passionate."

"Shut the fuck up. She's mine." He turned and Mattie's smile was like a punch in the gut. He was never going to hear the end of this from the guys.

CHAPTER 21: Terry

Terry cautiously made his way toward Maggie. She stood in the parking lot, face flushed as she spoke on the phone.

"Yes, you can pick me up—"

"I'll take you wherever you need to go."

She glared at him. His hand itched to put her over his knee and paddle that bottom. It'd be soft and pliable. His cock began to harden. If he didn't have her soon, he'd be embarrassing himself in public.

"I'm at Mattie's—"

"Hang up the phone." He used his sternest tone.

She shifted away from him. "Machines. I'll be waiting." She hung up the phone, turning toward him. "Go away. I don't want to talk to you right now."

"Maggie, I brought your car here instead of the other garage because I know Mattie. He's a friend and I knew he'd tell me"—at her glare he amended—"you the truth about the car."

She clenched her jaw for a moment and then said, "I know you were doing what you thought was best and I appreciate all you've done for me but—"

"Let me help you with this." He stepped closer to her. "You need a car. I can loan you one of mine."

"No. You've done too much already and...I can't repay you." She cleared her throat. "I can take care of myself."

"I'm sure you can, but I want to do it. I have an extra car sitting in my garage and taking up space."

"Figures." She laughed but it was a pained sound and her eyes filled with tears.

"Honey." He pulled her into his arms. "I got you. It'll be okay."

"No, it won't." She clung to him, sobbing against his chest.

"It will. I promise. Let me help you." He rested his cheek against her head. She felt so good in his arms, warm and soft. He couldn't stop his dick from responding so he made sure that he kept his pelvis away from her. This was about getting her to trust him. Sex would come later, but hopefully, not much later.

"You've already helped me so much and for what? Some stupid cookies?"

"Hey," He lightly swatted her ass and she squeaked, her head snapping upward. Lord help him, a spark of passion danced in her hazel eyes. They were going to be so good together. "Don't say anything bad about those cookies. They were the highlight of my week."

"Really?"

"Yes." His hand rested on the small of her back. "That and seeing you." *Without those kids.*

She bit her lip and he leaned down. He had to kiss her. He'd die if he didn't. He'd literally perish on the spot. His lips met hers. She hesitated only a moment before opening for him.

She was so damn giving that he was rock hard in an instant. He pulled her against him.

"See what you do to me." He nipped her lip and kissed a trail across her neck and up to her ear. He had to have her. "Come home with me."

CHAPTER 22: Maggie

"I can't." The words came from Maggie's mouth automatically, but they weren't true. She could go home with Terry. The kids were gone. She didn't have to work.

"This can be whatever you want. One night. More. Come home with me tonight and then decide."

His lips were on hers again, swallowing her refusal and she let go, only for a minute. She needed this moment. She deserved this moment. She wrapped her arms around his neck and his large hands cupped her backside, pulling her into his erection. She melted against him. She wanted to go with him and forget about everything—money, her job and god help her, even her kids. She just wanted to be a woman who desired a man for a few short hours.

A car pulled up next to them. Terry broke the kiss and she almost cried. Reality was returning.

He reached behind him and pulled out his wallet, keeping her tight against his body. "She won't be needing a ride." He hollered to the Uber driver, holding out a couple of bills.

She dropped her arms, hiding her face against his shirt as the driver came over and took the money.

"Thanks, dude. Have fun," said the driver.

"This is so embarrassing," she mumbled against his chest.

His hand was still on her ass. "You're embarrassed about this?"

She nodded, inhaling the clean smell of laundry soap, some kind of expensive cologne and him.

"This is nothing." He put his wallet away and his other hand came to her ass, lifting her.

"What are you doing?" Duh, he was carrying her across the parking lot. "You can't do this." She stared up at his handsome face.

"Go for it, dude," said the Uber driver.

"Terry, everyone's watching." She was surprised his clothes weren't singed from the heat coming off her face.

"Ignore them. Put your arms around my neck."

She obeyed without thinking.

"Good rabbit." He put her on the ground and opened his car door. "Now, get in."

She hesitated. This wasn't like her, but what had playing it safe and doing what everyone expected done for her? She was a chubby, divorced mother of three who was beyond broke. Still, old habits didn't go away easily. "We shouldn't."

"We should." He grabbed her chin. "We definitely should."

"I don't know."

"Get in. We'll go to my house and talk."

"Talk?" She couldn't help but smile.

"It's not what I want to do but if that's what you need...what you want, it's what we'll do."

She could do that. She could talk and then decide. Right. If lying to oneself was a sin, she'd better go to confession. She almost laughed. She'd have a lot more to confess than a lie if she went home with him.

"You have to come with me to get the car." His eyes gleamed with challenge.

"I'm not taking your car."

"I'm not giving you the car. I'm loaning it to you."

She frowned. "What if I damage it? You know the kids will have to ride in it and kids are messy."

"We'll talk about it at my place."

"Okay." She got into the car. She could lie to herself and say that was why she was going.

He closed the door and walked to the other side. He started the car and drove down the road.

Maggie stared out the window. She couldn't believe she was doing this. She shouldn't be doing this.

"Don't start having second thoughts."

"I-I'm not but—"

"No, buts." He took her hand bringing it to his lips for a kiss. "I want you. I have since the moment you bumped into me at the Club."

"Why?"

"I have no idea."

"Oh." That was not the answer she'd expected.

"Don't get your feelings hurt. I told you that I'm honest. Would you rather I lie to you?"

"No. I guess not." But something like he found her eyes pretty or thought she was hot would've been nice.

"Good. Because I'll never lie to you."

That sounded like a good thing but a lie of kindness wasn't too bad.

Terry pulled into a neighborhood that was very affluent. She'd thought she lived in a nice area. It was nothing compared to this. He drove down the street and she stared out the window in awe.

The houses were gorgeous. The yards were huge and immaculate. A family headed toward their car. The kids raced down the driveway, carrying little suitcases. She gasped.

"What's wrong?"

"Nothing." Everything. That family was her family, except with a younger, prettier her.

David and her kids were getting ready for their trip. She'd known he wasn't hurting for money like she was, but she'd had no idea he lived in a neighborhood like this. Her lunch of toast and tea churned in her stomach. She was broke and he was living in luxury. She watched her children in the side mirror as Terry drove down the street. How long before her kids would be living with him full-time? How long before he took her to court so he could have custody of their kids? How long before she was alone?

Terry turned down another street and pulled into a driveway, pressing a button on his phone and opening the garage door. His place was a beautiful, two-story, red brick house. He parked his Mercedes next to a blue Volvo. His garage was cleaner than her house. He got out of the car.

She didn't move. If she went into that house, they were going to have sex. Her body screamed, *What are you waiting for? It's been so long. Too long. You like him and he's got the biggest cock you've ever felt.* She flushed. Her body was crude but accurate. Still, her brain argued that this meant nothing to him. As much as she'd like to believe that this was just sex for her too, it wasn't. She liked him and that wasn't good. She needed to get her life together without a man before she leaned on another one. Plus, what if David found out? Would this give him ammunition if he wanted custody of the kids?

He opened her door. "Maggie." He held out his hand.

She caught a whiff of his cologne—it was rich and dark, like him.

He crouched down so he was looking in her eyes. "I promise that this is whatever you want it to be."

"You swear, you'll let me decide?" She didn't know why she asked. It didn't matter. She already knew what she was going to do. David wouldn't find out if it were only this one time. He was going on a weekend trip with their kids and all she had planned was going home to her empty house filled with boxes and sadness.

"Yes." His lips were thin. He wasn't happy about that, but he'd do it.

"Just this once." She took his hand.

His dark eyes gleamed, "Whatever you say." He helped her out of the car. "But I give you leeway to change your mind."

"I won't." She couldn't. It wasn't worth the risk to her kids or her heart.

CHAPTER 23: Terry

Terry opened the door and followed Maggie inside, his eyes on her ass. He wanted to grab her and fuck her against the door, but his little rabbit was too timid for that. Later, she'd trust him enough to follow his lead. He closed the door and she jumped.

The old dog he'd adopted from Nick trotted over to them and he reached down to rub Beast's ear.

"You have a dog?"

"Yes." It was insulting that his friends and now, Maggie were surprised that he liked dogs. He was crass and could be a jerk but who didn't like dogs?

Maggie held out her hand and the dog sniffed it and then nudged her for attention. "What's his name?"

"Beast."

"Beast?" She grinned. "He doesn't look like a beast. He's a sweetheart." She bent so she could pet the dog and Beast rested his head against her chest.

Suddenly, he was jealous of his dog. He wanted his face

pillowed on her breasts. "Not like vicious beast, but lazy beast. Good for nothing beast." He scratched the dog's head, letting his fingers trail down the dog's muzzle and closer to her gorgeous tits.

"Well, I think he's sweet." She stood, eyeing him suspiciously.

"He is and so are you." Normally, he'd offer his partner a drink to ease the tension but he was a little leery that if he left her to her thoughts too long, she'd change her mind. He walked up behind her and put his hands on her shoulders, running them down her arms as he leaned forward and kissed her neck. "Relax."

"I'm...sorry." She stepped forward, away from him. "I-I don't think I can do this. I thought I could. I wanted to but..."

Damn. He should've fucked her in his car. Mattie wouldn't have said anything. The mechanic actually had a spot in the back of his lot just for that. According to him, women who fucked mechanics liked to do it in cars. "Don't be sorry." He moved toward her but she took a step back so he adjusted his destination and walked into the living room. He poured two drinks—his scotch and a glass of wine for her.

"I should go."

"Nonsense. Let's talk first and then I'll take you home." Or to heaven, he prayed it'd be the latter. He moved over to her and handed her the wine.

"I shouldn't."

"One glass isn't going to hurt you."

"No, but—"

"I'm not trying to get you drunk so I can have my way with you." He grinned. "I like my women cognizant and completely willing, eager actually."

She flushed and he chuckled.

"Sit and we can talk about this like adults."

"Okay." She sat on the edge of one of the chairs in the living room.

"Why are you scared?"

"I'm not scared."

Liar. She was terrified. "Do you know anything about dominance and submission?"

Her eyes widened. "A little. That's with whips and stuff, right?"

"It can be." He watched her closely. He'd planned on fucking her for a few weeks before they'd try any of those things, but she'd liked the swat he'd given her in the parking lot. He'd never met a more natural submissive, even if she were fighting it at the moment. He took a sip of his drink. "But it's more about control."

"Yeah, the dom has it all."

"No. The real power belongs to the submissive." That was true to a point. A good dom knew how to train a sub so that she or he willingly gave up control and just rode the waves of pleasure.

"Right. I've seen *50 Shades of Grey*."

"And who had the true power in that story? She did. She wrapped Grey around her little finger."

"Yes, but that was the fiction part. I doubt that happens in real life."

Usually not, but he decided to remain silent on that one. His little rabbit thought she'd be happier as a fox. He'd give her some rein while showing her that she was perfect as she was.

"I'm a dom."

Her hand trembled slightly as she took a big gulp of wine. "That settles it, because I'm not a submissive."

"Of course not." Oh, she was. "But wouldn't you like to be...to try it?"

"No. I let David do whatever he wanted and..." She took another drink of her wine. "This is really good." She drank more, not wanting to finish her sentence.

She didn't need to say the words. Her ex had hurt her badly—her self-esteem, her confidence in herself and as a woman. It was time to start fixing all that. "I'm glad you like it. I bought it for you."

"You did? Why?"

"Because I want to be your dom but before you compare me to David again, listen to what a good dom does and is." Now, he had to sell it and then she'd be putty in his hands.

CHAPTER 24: Maggie

Why did these things happen to her? Maggie needed to change her life, take care of herself instead of always relying on a man and the first guy she was attracted to was a dominant— the exact wrong kind of guy for the new Maggie.

Terry said, "A good dom, one who's worthy of you—"

"I'm not a submissive." She wasn't going to wear a dog collar and let him tie her up or spank her. She shifted on her seat, trying to ease the throbbing between her thighs. She'd been curious about kinky sex ever since reading *Fifty Shades of Grey*.

"Takes care of his sub," continued Terry.

He went on as if she hadn't spoken, as if she didn't matter. It was exactly like David had treated her. She wasn't starting a relationship or even a fling with another self-absorbed asshole. She had her kids to think about. If David ever found out about this, he might take them away, especially if Terry were into that kinky stuff.

"He sees to her needs. All of them. Both in the bedroom

and out of it." His hungry eyes roamed over her body.

"I don't need you to take care of me." She wasn't falling into that trap again.

"Of course, you don't but wouldn't you like me to? Just for a little bit." He leaned forward. "Here, in this house, you'll be mine. You'll do what I say and I'll take care of everything. You won't have any worries."

"What about making you happy? Isn't that the worry of the submissive?"

"No. The sub obeys and that makes the dom happy. It's very simple. All you have to do is what I tell you. Nothing more and nothing less. All decisions are gone. All choices are made by me." He stood and walked toward her.

She sank back into the chair. It was like watching a predator—a tall, strong, sexy predator—approach except he wasn't going to kill her. He was going to make her feel alive, like a woman again.

He knelt before her. "All you have to do is relax and I'll take care of everything." His hands were on her knees, sending heat rushing through her body. "Forget about the car." He leaned forward and kissed her, a light brushing of his lips on hers. "Forget about the job you hate."

"H-how do you know I hate my job?"

He smiled. "Because I know you. Your job isn't a career. It's a means to an end. You'd rather be home taking care of your house, your children." He kissed her again, his hands sliding back and forth on her thighs going farther up with each pass. "Forget about your ex and money problems. Forget everything." Now, his lips were near her ear. "Doesn't that sound good."

She nodded. It sounded perfect and she wanted it—this

moment of nothing but the feelings he stirred inside her. Here, she could shed her responsibilities and just be a woman with desires.

"Say it, Maggie. I need to hear you say it."

"Yes."

"Yes, Master."

"Master?" She didn't like that.

"You may call me sir, if you prefer that over master." He nipped her ear. "Just in here. Just with me."

It didn't mean anything. It wouldn't hurt anyone and his lips felt so good. "Yes, Sir."

CHAPTER 25: Terry

Terry almost yelled in triumph but instead he stood, giving Maggie one last kiss.

"Where are you going?"

"To get you another drink." He took her glass from her hand and headed for the bar.

"No. Thank you. One's enough."

He turned and stared at her. "Rule number two, never question your master."

"There are rules?" She sounded appalled.

He chuckled. "A few but they're simple." He moved to the bar and filled her glass, bringing it back to her. "Rule one is always obey your master."

"And rule two is never question your master." She took the drink from him.

"I knew you'd be a quick study."

"It sounds like a cult."

He leaned down, bracing his hands on either side of her chair, letting her feel how much bigger he was than her. "A cult of pleasure between you and me."

"Are there other rules?" Her eyes darkened.

"Yes, but we can save them for another time."

"Terry..."

"Sir or Master, Maggie."

"Sir, wait."

He straightened. He wanted to punish her for her disobedience but she wasn't ready for that yet. "If you want to break out of the scene, you need to use your safeword."

"Scene? Safeword? I don't even know what those are. Am I not going to be safe?"

"I'll never hurt you more than you can stand."

"You're going to hurt me?" Her eyes darted to the door and she started to stand.

He leaned down and kissed her. Her mouth was lush and sweet like the wine. He deepened the kiss, savoring her taste for another moment before breaking away. "Trust me."

"I'm trying, but I don't want you to hurt me."

"You liked it when I swatted your ass." He kissed her again and her body softened with his attention, preparing for his hardness and strength. All he wanted was to sink into her and lose himself in her heat, but he forced himself to break the kiss. "That's all I'm talking about. Pain like when I spanked you. Pain that gives pleasure."

"Oh," she said against his mouth.

"Pick your safeword." He needed to get this game going or he was going to come in his pants.

"Uhm, I have no idea what it should be."

"Something you can't imagine saying while we play."

"Play?"

"Yes," he almost purred. "Red is a common one. It means to stop. Yellow means to slow down."

"Okay. We can use them."

"Perfect." He kissed her again, drawing her bottom lip into his mouth and nipping it before he broke away and sat on the chair across from her. She looked perplexed and that was perfect—keep her guessing, on edge and she'd come like never before. "Finish your wine."

"Ah...Red."

His jaw clenched. He'd never trained an innocent. Maybe, it wasn't worth it. His dick, which was pressing painfully against his trousers, assured him it would be. "Yes."

"I want to make sure you understand that this will only be a one-time thing."

"Whatever you decide." That wasn't going to happen. Once would not be enough for him and he'd make sure it wasn't for her either.

"Okay." She sipped her wine. "We can start again." Her face heated.

"Finish your wine."

"I am."

"Yes, Sir, is the answer."

"Is that all I can say?"

"No, but saying '*I am*' hints of disobedience."

"But I was doing what you said." Her lips pursed in confusion.

He wanted to command her to get on her knees and open for him as he slid his dick into that warm, wet heaven. "Do it faster. I want to see you naked."

"Oh." Now her face was on fire and he had to know if the

flush went all the way to her breasts. "Finish it."

She gulped down the wine, and his dick grew more at her eagerness to obey.

"Put your glass on the table and stand up."

She did, her hands fluttering nervously by her sides.

"Take your hair out of the ponytail."

She removed the rubber band, dropping it onto the table near the glass.

"Hold your hair above your head and let it fall down."

She obeyed. His gaze raked over her large breasts as the shirt pulled tight across them. They were luscious and he needed to see them. Her hair, the riot of curls, cascaded over her shoulders, a few strands covering her breasts.

"You are glorious. Those curls. I can't wait to wrap them around my fist and pull back your head as I fuck you from behind."

Her eyes were as wide as saucers. She must've never had anyone talk dirty to her but by the flush on her face, she liked it. A lot.

"Take off your shirt."

"Ah…"

"Yes, Sir," he reminded her.

"Yes, Sir." She looked down at her hands as she unbuttoned her shirt. Her skin was smooth and white with a little mole on her left breast that showed above her bra. Her tits were large and flushed a lighter shade than her face.

"Beautiful."

She dropped her shirt to the floor.

"Your bra too."

She started to protest but closed her mouth. His little

rabbit was learning. She reached behind her back, causing her breasts to spill forward as she unhooked her bra. She held it in place for a moment and then looked up at the ceiling as she let the cloth slide off her body.

"You're fucking gorgeous." His dick was screaming for him to let it out to play, but he wanted to take her through some paces. "Come here. I need to reward you for your obedience."

CHAPTER 26: Maggie

Maggie couldn't believe she was doing this. She'd been naked with David more times than she could count, but this was different. There was nothing David-like about Terry.

Her and David's relations had always been them together, not her across the room obeying his every command. It was wrong and yet so right. She was already wet and aching. She'd never admit it, but when he'd talked dirty, she'd almost orgasmed. She was still close. All she needed was a touch and those words and she'd break apart.

"Come here, little rabbit."

She had no idea why he called her that, but she was starting to like it. She was like a rabbit, scared and small but he was going to protect her. Guide her. She stopped in front of him, his dark eyes on her breasts.

"Offer one to me."

"What?" She couldn't have heard him right.

He dragged his gaze up to her face. "Don't question me."

"Sorry, Sir." There must be something wrong with her

because calling him sir made her even wetter.

"Do as you're told."

She lifted one of her breasts. It was soft and heavy in her hands—not as firm as she'd like and she prayed he didn't mind. She bent toward him, keeping her eyes averted. Her entire body was on fire, desire waging war with embarrassment. He ran his finger across her nipple. His touch was even warmer than her skin and when he pinched her softly, she gasped, her legs shaking with need. David had played with her breasts but it was nothing like what this man was doing to her.

"You liked that. Good, because I like getting rough." His hot breath stroked across her skin.

She wanted to grab his head and pull him to her, but she was pretty sure that wasn't allowed.

"Sit on my lap."

She turned to sit down but his hand caught her hip.

"Not like that." His dark eyes gleamed with amusement.

Her gaze dropped to his pants and he was more than aroused. Her mouth was suddenly dry as she put her hands on his shoulders.

He grabbed her hips, stopping her from straddling him. "First, take off your pants."

She kicked off her shoes. Her knees trembled as her fingers went to her button. This was it. If she did this, there was no turning back. She hadn't been with anyone but David in almost forever.

"Maggie, listen to me. Let everything else go except what I tell you. Nothing else matters in here."

It sounded so primal and so lovely, an escape from the hell that had become her life. She could turn it all over to him for a few hours. He could decide everything for her. She'd have no worries, no fears, nothing but his voice, his body and…Her eyes dropped to his cock which had been big before but now was huge. She wanted to feel him inside her, filling her, making everything disappear except him and her.

Her hands skimmed over her soft, round belly as she unbuttoned her pants. She wasn't in the best shape. He had to be aware of that from seeing her in her clothes, but it wasn't the same as her naked body. She'd had three kids. She had cellulite and flab. She didn't want to do this. Not like this—out in the open, in the light. "Uhm, what if we went to your bed or—"

"No."

She frowned. He hadn't even let her finish. "Then how about we turn off the lights?"

"No." He raised his dark eyes from her hands, pausing for a long moment on her breasts before meeting her gaze. "I gave you an order."

"Terry, please. I'm—"

"Sir." His voice was like sandpaper, raspy and hoarse.

"Please Sir, may we turn off the lights?"

"No."

"I don't…"

He stood, his chest so close he almost brushed against her breasts when he breathed. He grabbed the back of her neck, tipping her head so she looked at him. "Obey."

"I-I can't." She wanted to, but she couldn't.

"Why?" His face softened.

"I'm…I'm fat," she whispered. He had to know, but admitting it was so embarrassing.

Ellis O. Day

He frowned, his hand moving to her chin. "You're lush."

That made her feel a little better but..."You haven't seen me without my clothes."

"And whose fault is that?" One side of his mouth turned up in a smile.

"I want to do this. I want to obey but..."

"You are the sexiest woman I know." He swatted her ass and walked across the room. He grabbed the wine from the bar and refilled her glass.

"I thought you liked your women sober." She took the drink from him, thankful for the liquid courage.

"I do, but I think this will help you." He kissed her nose as his hands skimmed up her stomach to her breasts. "And I'm your master. It's my job to make sure you're happy and"—his fingers traced her nipples, causing them to harden almost painfully before he squeezed them—"satisfied."

She moaned, her back arching toward his touch, but he dropped his hands and sat on his chair.

"Finish your wine and then take off your pants."

She gulped down the drink. It helped but she still didn't want to stand before this man, who looked like a gorgeous Greek statue, in all her chubby glory.

"You're beautiful, Maggie and I want to see you."

She stared at her feet as she grasped the zipper of her pants.

"Look at me."

She closed her eyes for a moment. This was going from bad to worse. She didn't want to see his face when he got his first look at her body.

"I've given you some leeway because you're new at this,

but if you don't look at me now, I'm going to paddle your ass and not let you come."

Her eyes shot to his face. "What do you mean by that?" She orgasmed when she orgasmed.

"You'll see." His mouth curled in a smirk. "I'm going to enjoy bringing you close to release and then backing away. Making you beg me to let you come."

"You'd do that?" With David he just did his thing and she had to hope he hit the spots that she liked. When they'd first married, he'd seemed to try but over the years, it was more about his enjoyment than hers.

"Absolutely. Over and over again."

It sounded horrible and wonderful at the same time.

"Take off your pants and look at me while you do it."

She lowered the zipper, praying the desire in his eyes wouldn't turn to horror when he got his first glimpse of her cellulite and thick thighs. She stopped. The zipper had come to the end of its path.

His breathing was harsh and heavy as he stared at her. He raised his eyes from her hands to her face, one brow lifting. It was a non-verbal command and she understood. She'd delayed as long as she could. She grabbed the waistband and pushed down her pants. His eyes followed their descent and then back up to stare at the juncture between her thighs. Thankfully, she'd worn a decent pair of panties. They were white with a little lace. They weren't the sexiest thing but they were better than the grannie panties she sometimes wore to help keep her tummy in place.

"The underwear too." His eyes never moved.

There was nothing but lust on his face—no disgust, no

distaste at her body. She shivered as his dark gaze heated the flesh between her thighs like a smoldering fire. She shoved the panties down, letting them pool at her feet.

"Come here." He raised his gaze to hers.

She inhaled sharply at the raw desire in his eyes. To this man she wasn't fat or a mother, she was a woman he wanted. She stepped closer, feeling sexy for the first time in years.

"You are Venus." His eyes raked over her, leaving fissures of heat in their wake.

She blushed. She wasn't but she was glad he thought so. His eyes devoured her, but he remained still. His only movement was his chest rising and falling and his hands on his thighs, clasping the cloth of his pants as if trying not to reach for her. He should stop fighting. She wanted those large hands on her, exploring and caressing. She needed to feel his touch deep inside, stroking and coaxing. She shifted, trying to ease the ache inside of her. If he didn't do something soon, she'd touch herself—well, she wouldn't in front of him, but she wanted to.

He inhaled deeply, nostrils flaring. She closed her eyes. *Please don't let him say anything about a smell.*

"Look at me."

She opened her eyes.

"Why are you embarrassed?"

"How did you—"

"I know your body. I've studied you since the night we met."

"It's nothing." She was not going to talk about this.

"Tell me or I'll spank you."

Her eyes darted to his face. Would it hurt if he hit her or would it be more pleasure than pain?

"The truth. Now." His hand flexed. "Always, the truth between us. Nothing is embarrassing in here. There's nothing you can't do or can't tell me."

"I was afraid you'd say something about...you know, when you inhaled."

"Your scent?" He seemed amused and it was pissing her off.

"Yes, Terry. We all smell. Sex smells."

"Yes, Sir and sex smells wonderful." He moved his face toward her pussy. "You smell wonderful. Delicious actually."

She stepped back. David had been disgusted by oral sex—the giving part not, of course, the receiving.

"Get over here." His lips were thin lines of displeasure.

"I don't like...You don't have to...I don't want you to." God, she was a mess. She had no idea what she wanted. Her body screamed that it did want his mouth on her—there, but her brain said no, it was disgusting.

He grabbed her wrist. "You don't get to decide. I do. Remember?"

She nodded. That was right. He decided what he wanted, what she'd like. The tension fled like a wisp of smoke in a storm. She was free from decisions and second guesses. "Yes, Sir."

"I wanted to worship your breasts." His eyes roamed over her. "They are glorious but I think you need a lesson in obedience."

Her heart went into overtime. He wasn't actually going to spank her, was he? Her most private parts throbbed with excitement.

He stood. "Sit."

She sat in his chair, the warmth from his body lingered and

she snuggled against the cushion, inhaling his cologne.

He knelt in front of her. "Spread your legs."

"What? I mean, what Sir?" She couldn't do that. It'd be like asking him to...and she just couldn't do it.

"You heard me. Obey or I won't let you come."

She wasn't sure he'd have a choice. Her skin tingled in anticipation—one touch, one breath might be enough to send her flying to her release.

"Now, Maggie."

His deep tone slid inside her, taking over her body. Her legs dropped open a bit. He bent, his dark head contrasting with her pale skin. His mouth was hot and wet on her knee. His lips trailed upward as he spread her legs farther apart, making room for his large shoulders. His hot breath wafted over her core, caressing her, heating her. Her head dropped against the chair and she closed her eyes, feeling nothing but him—his hands, rough and strong holding her legs apart, his shirt, soft and gently scraping against the sensitive skin of her inner thighs, his mouth inches away from where she needed it.

"So beautiful." His fingers skimmed across her pussy, soft and fleeting. "And wet. So wet, for me. You like being my sub don't you."

Her hips arched toward him and he chuckled. She'd be embarrassed later, but right now, she needed him to touch her, really touch her. She moaned as he stroked her, his fingers firmer, harder, better, but not enough. He teased around her clit, never touching her there or inside—never going where she wanted him.

His finger stopped, resting lightly on her mound. "Answer me."

"What?" She leaned up, looking at him. She had no idea what he'd asked.

He frowned at her, his dark brow arching in expectation. "What, Sir?"

"I asked if you liked being my sub." His tone was firm but there was humor mixed with desire in his eyes.

"Yes, Sir." A smiled teased her lips. She liked this very much.

He grabbed her legs and pulled her forward until her butt was almost hanging off the chair. "That's better." He kissed her inner thigh—first one and then the other before putting them over his shoulders.

"Stop. You can't." This was beyond embarrassing. She was wide open. He could see everything. Everything.

"I can do whatever I want to *my* sub." He swatted her ass.

She squeaked as the sting from his hand seemed to echo through her body, settling between her legs. Right where his mouth lingered, so close but not touching. Fortunately, his fingers started working their magic again, rubbing and caressing her, making her body hum. Her head fell back. She no longer cared how she looked. All she cared about was that he didn't stop. Not yet. Not when she was so close. Her hips rolled with his fingers, following his touch.

"Can't I?" His lips brushed against her as he spoke.

"Yes." She wasn't sure what he was talking about but yes was the exact right word for what she was feeling.

"Yes, Sir." He ran his tongue along her crease, rough and wet and hot.

"Oh...god..."

"I suppose that'll work too." He buried his face in her cunt, licking and sucking, teasing and stroking.

It was too much. Her hands clasped the arms of the chair and then somehow made it to his head, clinging to him as his tongue fucked her. His large hands cupped her ass, holding her like an offering for him to feast upon.

"Look at me." His voice rumbled through her and she leaned up.

That was all it took. That one sight—her legs splayed over his large shoulder, still covered in his white work shirt, his dark head buried between her thighs as his tongue slide in and out of her while his finger rubbed her clit. Her body tensed.

"Oh...god..." She came, her hips rocking and her legs clasping his head as her hands tangled in his hair.

CHAPTER 27: Terry

Terry pulled Maggie's thighs from his shoulders, kissing one and then the other before putting them down and sitting back on his feet. God, she was sweet and so fucking eager. He wiped his face with his sleeve. She was limp on the chair, her hair a riotous mess of curls around her and her face and chest flushed from her orgasm. "I should punish you for coming."

"What?" Her eyes fluttered open as she lifted her head.

"But I hadn't told you that rule." He should've gone over all of them, but he'd been waiting to have her for too long. "So instead, I'll just fuck you."

"Yes, go ahead." She closed her eyes, relaxing back on the chair.

He couldn't help it. He laughed. "Oh, don't think you'll be a languid participant." He leaned over her, letting her feel how much bigger he was than her, how much at his mercy she was. When in reality, he wouldn't do anything she didn't want or wouldn't like.

"No. Of course not." She stared up at him, her hazel eyes

filled with sparks of green and gold. "Wh-what you did was lovely. Now, it's your turn."

"Damn straight." His mouth came down on hers.

She was so giving and willing. She opened immediately and let him ravage her. She wrapped her legs around his thighs, pressing against his erection. He moaned in her mouth. He had to have her, but he wanted her eager for him, not just willing to let him use her body to rut his way to orgasm. He pulled away and she didn't fight him.

"Not like this."

"Not like what?" She was confused and that was perfect.

"Like this." He picked her up and turned her around so she was kneeling in front of the chair. He pressed on her back.

"What are you doing?" She struggled against him.

He had her attention now. No more numbness from orgasm. "Sir and don't question me."

"Okay." She stopped struggling and let him lower her until her face rested on the cushion.

He adjusted her legs so they were spread wide, her white ass an offering to him. "Yes. Just like this." His hand caressed down her spine to her voluptuous rear. Fuck, he was going to explode.

"Terry...Sir...I...I'm not sure I like this."

The quaver in her voice made it clear that she was uncomfortable about her body again and he wouldn't allow that. It was a crime. She was a goddess of old—round and ripe, ready to be a feast for a poor mortal man like him.

"I'm sure." He leaned over her, his lips at her ear. She shivered and he grinned. "Trust me. You'll like this. You already like this."

"Ah…"

"You're wet again, aren't you? You can feel the ache, the emptiness inside you waiting for my cock, can't you?"

Her body trembled and she nodded.

"Say it, rabbit. I need to hear the words."

"Yes, Sir."

"Yes, Sir what?"

She turned, trying to see him. He grinned against her ear. She had no idea what he wanted her to say.

"Are you wet for me?"

"Yes…Sir."

"Do you ache"—his fingers traveled between her thighs to her pussy, tapping her—"here, for me?"

"Oh…"

"Say it." He moved his hand away.

"Yes, Sir."

"Say it. All of it."

"I can't talk like that." The scarlet hue of her embarrassment was traveling from her cheeks toward her shoulders.

"You can and you will." He ran his finger over her clit, teasing with light caresses and then pressing down until her ass wigged against him. He couldn't help it. He shifted so she rubbed against his cock. "Fuck, that feels good."

"Yes." She gasped as she pushed against his hand.

If he didn't watch it, she'd come again. He slowed, his fingers teasing her folds. "Say it, rabbit. Tell me what you want. Tell me what I do to you."

"Please…Sir, please." She wiggled her ass more and he groaned. "Take me. Do it."

His jaw clenched as he forced himself to sit back on his feet, to leave that haven of warmth and softness, that hot piece of heaven calling to him. "That's not good enough."

"What?" She started to sit up, but he put his hand on her back, holding her in place.

"Stay." He took off his tie. "I want to hear the words, Maggie." He grabbed her wrists and pulled them behind her back.

"Terry, what are you doing?" She was trying to see over her shoulder.

"Tying you up." He wrapped the tie around her wrists in an intricate knot, dragging out the process of confinement because it'd make her that much more tense, more nervous and more turned on.

CHAPTER 28: Maggie

"Tying me up? No. You can't do that." Maggie had never been tied up. She'd never wanted to be tied up. She wiggled but he had ahold of her wrists, keeping her face against the cushion.

"Yes. I can." He secured the restraint. "How's that feel?"

She felt helpless and horny. The ache between her legs was almost pain. She needed release and she couldn't even take care of it herself. She was at his mercy.

He leaned over her again, filling her world with his heat, his scent, his body. "Too tight?"

"I don't know about this." She tested her wrists. The bindings were secure but didn't bite into her skin.

"I do." He kissed her neck, his mouth hot and wet and then he nipped her.

She gasped but his tongue soothed the sting, making her melt like ice cream in the oven.

"How does this feel?"

"It's fine. Not too tight." She shifted forward a little so her pussy pressed against the chair. He was taking too long. She needed something, anything touching her down there.

"That wasn't what I asked this time, but I think your actions tell me all I need to know." He grabbed her hips, moving her away from the chair.

"No."

He wrapped her hair around his hand, pulling up her head. "Don't tell me no. Use your safeword if you need to, but don't tell me no. Understand?"

"Yes...Sir." She had no idea why, but the slight sting on her scalp made her even hotter. She was helpless. He had all the power, all the control.

"Good." He let go of her hair, gently pushing her head back to the chair. "I'm going to take off my shirt now" His voice was rich and dark, delicious.

"Yes." She wanted to feel all that hot, male skin around her.

"That's it, Maggie, talk to me."

He leaned away and there was the sound of clothes being removed and then he was back. The top half of his body hot and smooth, setting her skin on fire. She bit her lip to keep from moaning.

"What do you want me to do now?"

She wanted him to take her, make love to her, but she wasn't going to say that. "You're the master. Aren't you supposed to tell me?"

He stilled and she bit her lip again. That wasn't very sub-like, but she'd felt his erection earlier. He was rock hard and ready. No man walked away in that condition but he leaned away from her.

"Ter...Si—"

His hand landed on her ass with a slap.

"Ouch! Hey!" She tried to sit up, but his other hand captured her neck, keeping her against the chair.

"Don't question your master."

"S-sorry." She could say Red and end this, but his hand was caressing her ass where he'd hit her and his strong fingers felt so good.

"I'll let you off easy tonight, rabbit." He grabbed her thighs, spreading her legs wider before kneeling between them. "But we need to go over the rules and then you'd better behave or I'll have you over my knees."

"Yes, Sir." She wiggled, rubbing against him. She was on edge. She needed to come.

"The correct answer is 'thank you, Sir'." He swatted her again.

This time she gasped but it wasn't from the pain. That slap had made her pussy clench, sending pleasure shooting through her body.

"You like that don't you?"

She bit her lip.

"Answer me, rabbit."

"Yes, Sir." She closed her eyes. This was so embarrassing.

"Good girl." He leaned over her. "Now, you get a reward."

His hand skimmed over her abdomen and she cringed. He had to feel all that fat. She still hadn't lost the weight from having Davy.

"Your body is beautiful." His words were a whispered caress in her ear as his fingers stroked her. "I love how lush and full you are. How ready for me." He slid a finger inside her.

Her body clenched around him, but she needed more than

his finger.

"Say it. Tell me you want this."

"Yes, Sir, please." She more than wanted this. She needed this.

"Say the words." He slid another finger inside her and continued stroking.

"Yes, please. Make love to me."

His fingers stilled. "Do you love me, Maggie?"

"What?" This was awkward. She barely knew him.

"There's no way you do, but you want me." He began to move his fingers again and sparks flew behind her eyes. "So, call it what it is. You want me to fuck you." He slid another finger inside her. He was a large man and his fingers fit him. Three of them were stretching her in the best possible way.

"Oh…"

"Say it."

She never cussed. She had when she was younger but eight years of being around small children had changed her vocabulary.

"Say it or I'll stop." His fingers stilled, buried deep inside her.

"You can't. You haven't…"

"I haven't come, but I can do that without you. Or I can make you suck me off. Shove my dick in that pretty pink mouth of yours and fuck your face."

"Ohhh…ohhh." She moved her hips, clenching his unmoving fingers, finding her own release. His words were crass and dirty and god help her, she was coming again.
"There…please…right there."

"Oh no, you don't." He withdrew his hand and sat back on

his feet. "You don't get to come until I say so."

"Oh…" She moaned. "Please." She trembled on the chair; her body so tight with need she almost cried.

"That's a start." He stood.

"Where are you going?" She'd kill him if he left her like this.

"Stay right there." His large hand caressed her ass. "When I come back, you'd better be ready to tell me exactly what you want me to do or I'll leave you like this." His fingers trailed between her ass cheeks and lower, a whisper soft caress across her pussy. "Unfulfilled. Hungry for my cock."

CHAPTER 29: Terry

Terry strode into his bedroom, his dick straining at his zipper so much he was going to have permanent marks. He should've removed his pants a long time ago but then he would've fucked her. It wasn't time, not yet. Not until she said it. Not until she bent to his will. He wanted to hear all those dirty words describing the things they were going to do spilling from her lush lips. He grabbed a condom and another just in case and went back into the living room.

Maggie was exactly as he'd left her, like a good little sub. She was on her knees, her face resting on the seat of his large chair and her hair a tumble of curls, hanging around her head and shoulders. Her wrists were bound behind her back and her legs spread wide.

"You are so fucking hot." He could come just looking at her, stroking himself to completion and spending on her body. No. Maybe, later but this time, he needed to be inside her. He strode over to her and unzipped his pants. Her back arched at the sound. She was as eager for his cock as he was to give it to her. "Are you ready to do what I told you?"

"I-I don't—"

"Think about this, little rabbit." He let his pants drop and kicked them aside. "I can come with or without you. You're every man's wet dream—bound and bent, waiting for me. Wet for me." He moved between her legs and knelt. "So, either tell me you want me to fuck you. That you want this huge cock shoved so deep inside you that you won't be able to walk for a week, or I'll come on your back." He spread her ass cheeks and placed his cock between them, his hips thrusting on their own at the softness and heat of her body. "Oh fuck, you feel good." He moved his dick between her legs, sliding it across her pussy lips, teasing her and himself.

"Yes. Please, Terry." She was wet and hot, slick with desire.

"Say it." He'd let her slide on calling him Terry. He either needed to get inside her soon or he'd finish on her back and he wanted to feel her wrap around him, milking him until there was nothing left. He shifted so the strokes of his cock bumped against her clit. "Say it or I stop."

"Oh...yes...please...fuck me, Terry. Please, I want your cock inside me. Now."

"Fuck." Those words in her soft voice made his balls tighten and his dick twitch. He pulled back and she moaned.

"I said it. Please, don't stop."

"Condom." He grunted out the word as he slid it down his dick and moved back between her legs, stroking against her pussy and lubing his cock with her juices. He was a large man and even though she was ready, this would be tight.

"Please, Terry. Now." She wiggled and squirmed, rubbing against him.

139

Ellis O. Day

He positioned himself at her opening and slid inside, a little, giving her time to adjust to his girth. "You feel so fucking good." He pushed in a little more. It was heaven—tight, wet and hot.

"Oh…" Her face was flushed and she was panting.

"You okay?" He stopped, his chest heaving. He wanted to shove all the way inside and fuck her until he came, but he had to make this good for her. By the look on her face, right now, it wasn't good.

"You're…big."

"Yeah, and you'll love it." He bent, kissing her neck. "Just give me a moment." His teeth ground together as he forced himself to pull almost all the way out. His spine spasmed and he swore if his dick could talk, it'd be screaming obscenities at him for dragging it out of heaven. He slowly pushed back into her body before retreating once again. He repeated the motion over and over, going no farther than the first time. "Relax, baby." He skimmed his hand up and down her back. It was torture and bliss. Heaven and hell, but he had to keep going. He had to make it good for her. "That's it." He almost wept when she started moving with him. He shoved in a little deeper this time and she gasped but her body clung to him as he withdrew. "You like that, don't you?"

"Yes." Her eyes were closed and her lips parted, a soft rosy flush covering her cheeks.

"Fuck, Maggie." She was so tight and felt so right. He continued his slow thrusting, each time going a little deeper until he was finally in all the way. "You okay?"

She nodded but he could see a tear trailing down her cheek. He bent and she gasped as his dick repositioned inside of

140

her.

"Tell me when you're ready." He kissed the tear away.

"You can finish."

"No, little rabbit. You belong to me and this is how it works. I take care of you and then you take care of me."

"I'm fine." Her voice was shaky. She was far from fine.

He kissed her ear. "I don't want you to be fine. I want you to be hot and horny. Begging for my dick."

Her face flushed and he felt her tighten around his cock.

"You like it when I talk like that, don't you?" He gave a tentative thrust.

"Yes." It was a whisper.

"You also like my big dick stuffed inside your tight pussy."

"Yes."

"You liked my tongue in your pussy too, didn't you?" He thrust again and she moaned but it was a sound of pleasure. He closed his eyes. Soon. Soon, she'd be ready for fucking.

"Yes." She clenched around him as he withdrew.

"Are you ready to fuck, Maggie? Are you aching for me to fuck you so hard you shatter into a million pieces?"

"Yes. Please." She was rocking with him, following his lead.

"Thank god." He straightened and she gasped but it turned into a moan as he slid almost all the way out and then thrust back inside her until his balls rested against her ass. Her muscles tightened around his cock as she shoved against him. "You want to be fucked hard, don't you?"

"Yes." It was half-plea and half-moan.

"Say it." He grabbed her chin and lifted her head. "I want the words."

"Fuck me, Terry. Please, fuck me and make me scream."

"Shit." He almost came right then, but instead he let go of her chin and grabbed her hips, holding her in place while he slid into her, over and over. Her body tightened around his, clasping onto his cock. He gritted his teeth, trying to hold back his release but her moans weren't helping. They had turned into one long, keening sound of pleasure. She was almost there. He could feel trembles coursing through her, but he couldn't wait. He'd waited too long. "Now, Maggie. Come for me, now." He slapped her ass as he shoved inside her. She screamed, her body bucking and squeezing him. His balls tightened and his back stiffened as his hips thrust forward and stilled as he came. He dropped on top of her, his dick twitching and spurting inside of her.

CHAPTER 30: Maggie

Maggie had no idea how long she lay there. If it weren't for the pain in her knees and arms, she could've stayed forever with Terry's large body wrapped around her, protecting her. No, he wasn't protecting her, but he had given her the best orgasm...orgasms she'd ever had. "Terry."

"Hmm." He mumbled against her neck.

"My arms."

"Oh shit. Sorry." He lifted up and untied her wrists. He was still buried deep inside her but he wasn't hard anymore.

"Oh..." She groaned as feeling flooded back into her limbs.

"Let me." He rubbed her arms, his strong hands easing away the aches.

She sighed, resting her head against the chair. She should feel some embarrassment—kneeling naked on the floor, her face pressed against a chair—but she didn't. She didn't feel anything but satisfied and boneless. His fingers moved to her shoulders and she moaned. "Oh...god, that feels so good."

"I should be offended." He chuckled. "I think you're

enjoying this more than you did my cock."

"They're both nice." She smiled. He hated that word.

"Watch it." He swatted her ass playfully.

She tightened her inner muscles and the breath whooshed from his chest as his dick twitched inside her.

"So, my little rabbit wants more."

"Why do you call me that?"

"That's what I thought the first time I saw you." His hands worked their way across the muscles in her back.

"I'm not a helpless rabbit." She didn't like the metaphor. Especially since lately, she felt helpless and adrift in a storm of problems she had no way to solve.

"You sure looked like it that night. Face pale, eyes wide as you took in the scene." He laughed. "You were a little rabbit in a den of hyenas."

"Shouldn't it be wolves?" She tightened her inner muscles again, teasing his cock. She'd show him who the rabbit was.

"Nah. I'm the wolf. The rest of them are hyenas." He leaned down and kissed his way up her spine. "You're in my den now and a wolf knows exactly what to do with a rabbit."

"Yeah?" She clenched her muscles again, tightening around his hardening cock.

"Absolutely." He shifted, pulling out of her.

She moaned, her pussy throbbing, searching for its toy.

"Let's go to bed." He offered her his hand.

She took it and let him help her to her feet. The blood rushed to her legs and she swayed. He pulled her close, his large body, warm and strong, as he led her to the bedroom.

The room was as immaculate as the living room. Everything expensive, elegant and in its place. A huge bed sat in the center.

The wood was dark and heavy, the bedding tan and green to match the carpet and walls. There wasn't a hint of femininity to be seen.

He pulled down the covers. "After you."

She was suddenly shy. It was weird because they'd done so much but now, she was naked and crawling into a bed with this man she barely knew.

"You okay?"

"Yeah." She smiled at him. "It's just…I haven't shared a bed with anyone but my ex in over ten years."

"We can go to the couch if you're not ready."

"No. I'm more than ready." David hadn't wanted her. He'd left her and their life for someone else. She was ready to move on too, even if it were only for the night. She crawled onto the bed and flopped down on a pillow, tugging the sheet up and over her body.

He started to get in.

"Wait."

He stopped a curious expression on his face. "You do understand that we're going to share this bed, right?"

She laughed. "Yes, but I"—she knew her face was heating, but she didn't care—"didn't get to see you."

He grinned and held out his arms. "Feast your eyes." His gaze dropped to her lips. "You can feast with other parts of your anatomy later."

Her eyes traveled over his body. He was in excellent shape—wide shoulders, thin hips, muscular chest with a sprinkling of dark hair and the arrow that led her gaze to…"Oh, my. You're huge." There was no way that entire thing had been inside her.

He grinned. "I'm still growing right now, but I'll be at max soon if you keep looking at me like that."

"I can't believe that fit."

He climbed into bed and leaned over her. "It did and it's going to again."

"I don't know." Now that she saw it, she wasn't so sure she could handle that thing.

"I do." His lips came down on hers and that was all it took.

It was instinct. He demanded and she gave. She opened for him, letting him ravage her mouth. He shifted and she opened her legs too. She wanted this man and it'd fit before so it'd fit again. He grabbed her face, tipping her head and thrusting his tongue into her mouth, all gentleness gone.

"You drive me mad, little rabbit." He kissed his way down her neck to her breasts. "You have the most gorgeous tits I've ever seen." His tongue flicked her nipple.

It was hot and firm and she wanted more. She grabbed his head, holding him in place. He latched onto her nipple, sucking hard. Desire shot from her breast to her center and she thrust upward, offering more of herself, all of herself. He could do whatever he wanted as long as he didn't stop.

He broke away.

"Terry..." Her fingers still clutched his hair. She was probably pulling some out, but she needed his mouth back on her.

"Condom." He reached inside his nightstand and grabbed one, tearing it open and rolling it down his dick.

"That thing is huge." Bigger than before—a lot bigger. Panic wared with desire, making her throb even more. She reminded herself that it'd felt so good in the living room.

"Glad you like it." He smirked.

"I think you're going to ruin me for anyone else."

"Good." He grabbed her thighs and positioned them around his waist.

She locked her ankles, rubbing against his hardness and almost purring.

"Now, where were we?" He kissed her quickly and nibbled his way back to her breast, his teeth causing her skin to tingle in anticipation.

She held her breath, waiting to see if he'd nibble her there too. She had no idea if it'd hurt or if she'd like it, but then his mouth was on her nipple, sucking and licking, devouring her. Her head dropped back, a whimper slipping past her lips as she sunk into the mattress, her legs tightening around him and her hands holding his head in place. His teeth scraped across her nipple, dancing the edge of pleasure and pain. She arched her back, begging for more. He shifted, his dick pressing against her. He leaned on one arm, guiding himself to her opening. She gasped as he stretched her, fissures of pain sparking at his intrusion.

"Shhh." He kissed her mouth, his finger going between her legs and stroking her. "It's okay, baby. We'll go slow like last time." He kissed her again and his thumb teased around her clit as he slid deeper.

"Oh…" She gasped. He was all the way in now, throbbing and thick and god, she wanted more. "Please, Terry."

"Sir." He kissed her nose.

"Please, Sir."

"Say it." He held still, except for his thumb, teasing her tiny bud, coaxing the words from her.

"Fuck me. Please. Move." She no longer cared that a mother didn't say those words. Here in this bedroom, in this house with this man, she was a woman first.

"Whatever you want."

He kissed her quick as his hips pumped faster and faster—filling her, stretching her, touching her so deep that she trembled. His mouth latched onto her breast, sending desire shooting through her abdomen. Need pooled between her legs, spiraling higher and higher with each deep, hard slide of his cock. She closed her eyes, holding on to him. He was the only solid thing in her life. The rest was nothing more than sensation—glorious, wonderful sensation. "Oh...god...Terry..."

He bit down on her nipple and she exploded, her body holding onto him as she came. His hips rocked harder, each retreat making her clamp around him tighter, wanting him to stay and before she realized what'd happened, her body was on fire again and another orgasm rolled through her like a tornado. She screamed as she bucked against him.

CHAPTER 31: Maggie

Maggie was sprawled across Terry's chest. He must've moved her because the last thing she remembered he'd been on top and she'd just had the best orgasm in her life. She wiggled, loving the way his hard body felt below her and…He was still buried inside her body, flaccid but there.

"You're back." His tone was smug but she didn't care. After that performance he deserved to be smug.

"Yeah." She kissed his chest and his hand wandered slowly up and down her back. She should move. She was probably smashing the poor man, but she didn't want to go anywhere—ever.

"What time do you have to go home?"

She almost gasped. His words were like ice water dumped over her head. Apparently, he not only wanted her off his body; he wanted her out of his house. "Ah, you're right. I should go." She climbed off him, inhaling at the twinge of pain and loss as his dick slid from her body.

"Maggie?"

She sat up. Searching for her clothes. Damn, they were in the living room. She grabbed the sheet, covering herself as she climbed out of bed.

"What's the matter?"

"Nothing. I need to go." If she didn't get away from him, she'd cry. She hadn't expected a marriage proposal or anything but she also hadn't thought it'd be a "wham-bam-thank-you-ma'am" situation either. She took a step and the sheet didn't move. She tugged but he was lying on part of it.

"You have to go now?" He didn't move but his dark eyes studied her.

"Don't worry. I'll be out of here as soon as the Uber arrives." She gave up on the sheet and hurried from the room. He'd more than seen her body, so what difference did it make?

"Maggie..." He stood in the bedroom doorway.

"Don't. Please." She grabbed her underwear and pants from the floor. "It was fun. Thanks."

"Fun?" He strode forward, reaching for her.

"Don't. Don't touch me." She dodged him.

"Damnit. Sit down."

She started to sit but stopped. "I'm not your pet."

This time he did grab her, yanking her against his hard, bare chest. "But you are, little rabbit."

"Stop calling me that." She wasn't timid and helpless. She was a grown woman.

"No." His hands went to her ass, lifting her off the ground.

"What are you doing? Where are you taking me?" Her clothes slipped from her fingers as she wrapped her arms around his neck.

"Back to bed."

His erection pressed against her abdomen, rubbing with each long stride he took. Heaven help her, she wanted him again. "No. We can't. I'm not going to do this again."

He tossed her onto the bed and was on top of her before she could sit up. "Why? You enjoyed it. A lot." He grinned down at her, as he pushed her legs apart, positioning himself between them.

"Terry, please."

He shifted, so he was on her side, one leg, across hers, holding her in place. He leaned on an elbow. She turned away but he captured her face, forcing her to look at him. "Tell me what's bothering you."

"It's nothing."

"It's not nothing." He kissed her softly. "Tell me, so I can fix it."

"It's not you. It's me." She'd been a fool, again.

"Don't give me that shit."

"No. I mean, I shouldn't have expected anything." She wasn't young anymore and she had the body to prove it. Carrying a child took its toll and with the last one, no matter what she tried the weight wouldn't come off. He was rich, attractive, in excellent shape and had a huge penis. He could have anyone he wanted. She should be thankful for the quickie. She almost snorted. Right. Thankful to be reminded of exactly what she was missing.

"What are you talking about?"

"We had fun and now it's over. You made that perfectly clear."

"What? How did I make that clear?"

"You wanted me to leave."

"I did not."

"You said you wanted me to go." She wasn't crazy. He had said that. "Just because you're horny again don't pretend you didn't want me to leave." And that was exactly what she was going to do. She squirmed, but he was too heavy. "Let me up."

"No. You know the rules. Use the safeword if you need to"—he pressed himself more securely against her—"but I never...never said I wanted you to leave." He captured her face. "I don't want you to go."

"You don't?"

"No." He kissed her again and this one was a little deeper, a little darker.

"Then, why did you want to know when I had to leave?"

"Is that what your huff is about?"

"It's not a huff. You...you...It hurt. I know this doesn't mean anything to you but I..." She turned away. "I guess, I wanted it to be more than just a quickie."

"Maggie." His tone was amused.

"It's not funny."

"It is. I enjoy learning what sparks my little rabbit's temper."

"Stop calling me that."

"No."

She turned toward him and he was grinning. "You can't just say no."

"I can and I did." He trailed his hand down her cheek. "Now, tell me when you have to be home so I know how many hours I have left to fuck you."

Her breath hitched and a throb started between her legs. "You really want me to stay?"

"Yes." He captured her hand and put it on his dick. "See how much?"

"I do." She squeezed, loving the way his breath hitched.

"So, how long?"

She ran her hand up and down his length, stroking and squeezing. "I'd say very long." He was—long and thick and getter harder by the minute.

He laughed. "How many hours or minutes?"

"The kids are with their father."

"All night?"

She nodded.

"Excellent." The heat from his grin sizzled all the way to her toes.

CHAPTER 32: Terry

Terry stretched. His body weary in the best way. He'd fucked Maggie all night, but he still wanted more. She was soft and warm and so damn giving. He rolled over, leaning up on his elbow. She was curled on her side, facing the wall with the covers pulled up to her chin. That wasn't going to work. He grabbed the blankets, sliding them down and revealing her lush form.

He shifted closer–hard and ready for another round. He kissed her neck with soft little caresses of his lips and tongue, making his way to her ear. "You awake?" His hand wandered over her waist and up to her breast.

"Hmm," she moaned.

He shifted so his dick was cradled against her ass. She was so lush. He needed her now but their first night together was a little too soon for him start fucking her before she woke. He kissed her neck, pinching her nipple. "Come on, baby. Wake up."

"Hmm." She wiggled against him but she was still asleep.

He lifted her leg, positioning it over his. He reached between them, stroking his dick against her pussy. He groaned at the heat and the slick slide between her folds. "Wake up, Maggie, or my cock's going to be your alarm clock." His hand trailed over her abdomen to her pussy. He teased her clit with his fingers as his cock rubbed her folds. Her breathing grew uneven and her pussy was getting wetter. He needed to be inside her. "You awake? Please tell me you want this." He rocked against her, his dick sliding against her clit.

"Yes...Sir." She clasped onto his hand.

"Thank god." He leaned over and grabbed a condom. He put it on and rolled back, pulling her flush against him. "Lift your leg. Knee bent."

His dick almost exploded when she didn't even hesitate to obey. With her one leg up and bent at the knee she was wide open for him. He grabbed his cock, relishing the heat from her body as he rested it against her pussy lips but he didn't push inside. "Tell me what you want."

"You. I want you." She reached over her hip, grabbing his wrist and trying to guide him inside her.

"What part of me do you want?" He smiled against her ear. His little rabbit was so eager.

"Your cock. Give me your cock, Terry...Sir, please." Her voice was raspy with need.

"Fuck, yes. Say it again." But he couldn't wait. He slid into her and she stiffened. He stopped. "You okay?"

"Yeah. Just a little sore." She turned her head and smiled at him. "I haven't been this thoroughly used in...well, ever."

"Not used." He kissed her nose. "Never used."

Her smile grew wider.

"But whatever you call it, get used to it." He began to thrust in long, hard strokes. She started to roll back over. "Look at me while I fuck you." He needed to see her pleasure, what he did to her.

She turned, watching him as he pumped into her. Her eyes darkened and her lips, still red from their earlier activities, parted as small, breathy moans escaped.

"That's it. Fuck, Maggie. You feel so good." He grabbed her leg and lifted it higher, allowing him to slide farther inside. She was so tight and hot. His hips moved faster, the friction driving him toward release.

"Oh..." Her mouth opened and her eyes drifted shut.

"Look at me."

She opened them, but only halfway.

"You can't come yet."

"Please." She licked her lips.

"No. Not until I say." He slowed his pace, bringing her back from the edge. The passion cleared from her eyes, banked now, but still simmering. "There you are. Let's go again." He wrapped his arm under her knee and opened her wider. She moaned as he pushed into her. "So...fucking...good." He wasn't going to last long. He could slow down, but he didn't want to. He started fucking her faster and faster, the slide and tug making his balls tighten.

"Please...Terry...Sir."

"What?" He was fighting his own release but he needed her to beg him.

"May I come, Sir. Please."

"Yes." He shifted and pumped into her again and again as she moaned. Her body trembled and tightened around him, squeezing him tight and holding him inside. "Fuck," he groaned against her neck as he came.

CHAPTER 33: Maggie

Maggie opened her eyes, blinking in the semi-dark room. This wasn't her house and then she remembered. She'd had sex, lots of it, with Terry. She grimaced at the pinch of pain between her legs but it was so worth it. She'd never, ever had orgasms like she'd had last night. She rolled over to find her stud—correction, her temporary stud—but the bed was empty.

The curtains were drawn and the room was dark except for a little sunshine that peeked in from the bathroom. What time was it? She crawled out of bed but there was no clock. Her phone and purse were in the living room and so were her clothes. She couldn't walk out there naked. It was bad enough he'd seen her body at night. She wasn't going to parade around in her birthday suit in the stark, unforgiving light of day.

She reached for the sheet. One of his shirts was on the foot of the bed. There weren't any other clothes scattered around and it looked clean and unwrinkled. Maybe, he'd left it for her. She slipped it on. It was as long as a short skirt and the sleeves hung well past her hands. She wiped at her eyes. It was stupid.

It was only a shirt, but it made her feel cared for, wanted. If nothing else, he'd thought of her comfort and that was more than David had done in years. She rolled up the sleeves and buttoned it most of the way before going into the bathroom.

God, her hair was a mess—frizz and curls everywhere. Her makeup was mostly gone. She wiped the eye liner away and washed her face. She did her best to tame her curls, ending up twisting them into a very loose bun. There was only one toothbrush. It had to be Terry's. She wasn't brave enough to use it. David had hated it when she'd touched his stuff. She took the toothpaste and smeared some on her finger to brush her teeth.

She stared at the bathroom door. All that was left was to go into the living room. She hadn't had a morning after in forever and never like this. Besides for two high school boyfriends, with whom she'd never spent the entire evening, there'd only been David. They'd dated for months before they'd spent the night together. This thing with Terry was completely different. She barely knew him and the things he'd done...The things she'd let him do to her. Her body hummed and the ache between her legs became a little less pain and a little more desire.

She squashed it. It was the morning after and if he'd wanted sex, he'd have stayed in bed. Nope. Her fantasy had been fun, but it was over. She checked herself in the mirror one more time and then left the bathroom. She really had no choice. She couldn't hide in here forever. She walked into the living room and the smells of coffee and bacon slapped her in the face, making her stomach rumble.

"Good morning." Terry sat to the right of the bedroom at the dining room table, his laptop open and an empty plate nearby.

"Morning." She felt her face heat. This was so embarrassing. He looked immaculate as always. He was dressed in jeans and a T-shirt but he still looked unrumpled. She on the other hand looked like she'd just crawled out of bed, which she had—his bed.

"Hungry?" He stood.

"Starving."

"I bet you are." He grinned, his dark eyes trailing down her body, causing her nerves to tingle in anticipation. "Not yet. You need to eat first."

She wasn't sure if he were talking to her or himself so she didn't say a word.

"Sit. I'll get your breakfast."

"You don't have to. I can—"

"Sit." His eyes narrowed but one side of his mouth was tipped up in a grin. "I think we need to go over the rules. I never did get the chance to tell them to you."

"You had plenty of chances," she said as she sat.

"I did." He walked into the kitchen which was right next to the table so she could still see him. He wasn't wearing shoes or socks and even his feet were sexy, long and strong looking. "But you kept distracting me."

"Me?"

"Yes, you." He filled a plate with eggs, bacon and pancakes.

"What did I do?"

"You, my dear, are a cock tease." He carried the plate to her and put it down.

"I don't think I exactly teased you." She'd done whatever he'd wanted and had loved it. She grabbed a piece of bacon.

"Oh, you teased me all right, but you followed through like a good girl." He went back into the kitchen. "Coffee?"

"Please." She'd kill for a cup of coffee right now.

"Cream? Sugar?"

"Both, please." She took a bite of the pancake. "This is delicious."

"Glad you like it. Breakfast is the only thing I can cook." He put the coffee in front of her but didn't move.

"What?" She glanced up. His staring was making her nervous.

"Nothing." He went back to his seat and sat down.

"Is something wrong?" She wrapped the pancake around a slice of bacon and took another bite.

"No. I was going to make you sit on my lap while you ate."

"Oh." Her eyes darted toward his crotch even though the table blocked her view.

"Exactly. I would've ended up fucking you and although that would've been exceptional, I think you need to finish your breakfast. Build up your energy." He smiled. It was slow and full of heat as his eyes rested on the skin above her breasts. "Unbutton the shirt."

"Ah, I don't think that's a good idea." Not if she wanted to eat because her body was already melting for him. He was more addicting than chocolate.

He shook his head, feigning disappointment. "Listen closely. If you remember, rule number one is always obey your master."

"But we aren't—"

"Rule two is never question your master. Rule three, you must only come when I give you permission. Rule four—"

"Terry..." She needed to remind him that this wasn't going to happen again. She couldn't let it.

"What's the matter?"

"You know, I said last night that this was just a one-time thing. I mean, if you still want to...I can stay for a little while, but I have to leave soon. What time is it?"

His eyes narrowed. "Almost ten."

"Ten?" She shoved the rest of the bacon in her mouth and jumped up, taking a large gulp of her coffee. "I've got to go."

"What time do your kids come home?" He stood.

"What?" She grabbed her clothes from the couch where they were now neatly folded. She couldn't believe she'd slept this late.

"Your kids. What time to they get home?"

"Oh, not until Sunday around five." She headed for the bedroom. It was stupid, but she didn't want to change in front of him. It was too intimate somehow.

"Sunday? At five?" He followed, stopping her from shutting the door.

"Terry, please."

"What's your hurry?" He pushed past her.

"You want me to stay?"

"Yeah. Stay until Sunday." His head dipped and he glanced away, seeming vulnerable and her heart melted. "You can take the car when you need to go home."

The melting stopped. The man was infuriating. They both knew she hadn't come over here last night to discuss borrowing his car. "I'm not taking your car." She moved to the bathroom and quickly closed the door.

"Maggie, what are you doing?" He turned the handle.

"Unlock the door."

"No. I'm changing."

"So."

"I don't want to do that in front of you." She pulled on her underwear and pants.

He laughed. "I've seen everything you have." His voice darkened. "Hell, I kissed almost everything you have. I've had my tongue inside or on almost every body part except your ass. I was remiss in my attentions there."

"Stop it." Her face was beet red but worse than that, her legs trembled and she was starting to get wet as memories of all they'd done heated her body. She fastened her bra.

"Open the door."

She pulled on her shirt.

"I'll break it down."

"Don't bother." She opened it.

"Damn. You dress fast." He moved into the bathroom, stealing all the room and most of the air. "But I bet I can undress you faster."

She stared up at him. Her body softening as his hands moved to her hips.

"Good morning, Maggie." He bent and his mouth met hers. The kiss was warm and rich with the flavors of coffee and bacon.

She leaned against him as his hands moved to her ass and pulled her closer. He was hard and ready for her. She sighed. Who was she kidding? She didn't want to leave. "We have to make it quick," she said against his mouth.

"You don't give the orders." His kiss deepened as he lifted her and put her on the bathroom counter.

"Please, Te...Sir."

He unbuttoned her pants and lifted her up, peeling them and her underwear down her legs and off her body. He straightened, his eyes on the juncture of her thighs. "Spread your legs."

She couldn't believe she was doing this—right here in the bathroom, lights blaring—but she was. Her breathing increased as she opened for him, letting him see how wet she already was.

"Fuck, you're beautiful." His finger skimmed up her thigh and between her legs, caressing one side of her pussy.

His touch was soft and fleeting, teasing. Her eyes drifted shut as her hips followed his magical finger, seeking more.

"Open your eyes and look at me."

Her eyelids fluttered and she stared into his dark gaze.

He moved his finger over her clit, around and around, all the while watching her. "You like that, don't you?"

"Yes...Sir."

"Lift your shirt."

She did, no longer even thinking about disobeying.

"Now, your bra."

She did, letting her breasts bounce free.

He bent, taking her nipple in his mouth while his finger teased her pussy. His lips and tongue were magic, sucking and licking. Her hand tangled in his hair, pulling him closer while the other one grabbed onto his broad shoulder, skimming along his muscles. His arm came up under her knee, raising her leg as he bent. Her hands braced behind her as she watched his descent. He trailed kisses along her leg and up across the skin of her inner thigh. The coarse hair of his morning stubble rubbed against her. She'd have marks but the thought only made her wetter as his hot breath blew across her pussy. He looked up, holding her gaze as he spread her lower lips, his fingers long and rough against her sensitive flesh. He opened his mouth, his hot breath tickling and teasing, and then he licked her.

"Oh, god." Her body trembled, as much from the sight as his touch.

"Don't come until I give you permission." His words rasped against her, making her shake even more.

"Ter...Sir. Please." She couldn't not come. If she were ready, she came.

"If you're close say Yellow and I'll slow down." He licked along her sides and over her clit. His tongue, long and firm, thrust inside her before retreating and pressing against her clit for one quick moment. He repeated the pleasure, again and again.

She leaned farther back, her thighs clasping his head. His stubble scraped her flesh, adding to the sensations. He gripped her legs, forcing them apart, keeping her open for him. While his tongue was busy thrusting inside her, his finger teased her clit. It was too much. Too much feeling. Too much pleasure. She was so close. She wanted to come but he wanted her to wait.

"Yellow..." She panted. Her body wound so tight she was going to break apart as she stared at his dark head between her thighs.

He lifted his face, breathing heavily against her oversensitized flesh. "Good girl." He kissed her inner thigh. "Tell me when I can start again." But he didn't sit and wait for her to calm down, compose herself. He trailed hot opened-mouth kisses over her legs as one hand skimmed up her abdomen to her breast, squeezing and caressing her nipple with his thumb in teasing touches to entice but not to enflame.

She arched her back into his hand. She needed more. "Please. I'm ready, Sir."

His eyes darkened and he kissed his way between her legs, but this time, his finger slipped inside of her while his tongue teased her clit.

"Oh...oh....you...it...feels...so good." If he kept that up, she wasn't going to last long but her body wouldn't let her say Yellow. She'd betrayed it once and couldn't do it again. Not now. Not yet.

His lips surrounded her clit, pausing for one second before he sucked. At the same time, he shoved another finger inside her, bending them and thrusting fast and hard. That was it. Her fight was over. Her head dropped back and she moaned, her body shaking and clenching around him. He kept thrusting and sucking, making her orgasm spike and spiral again. She screamed, pressing against his face, begging him for more and more.

When there was nothing left but aftershocks, he kissed each thigh once more and straightened, wiping his face on a towel. "Look at me."

Opening her eyes was next to impossible. She had no muscles left. She was nothing but a heap of satiated flesh, but she struggled to do as he said and managed to peer up at him through a tiny opening. He was frowning at her.

"Did I give you permission to come?"

"No." She almost laughed but he didn't look like he was joking.

"No, what?"

"No, Sir but—"

"No excuses. I went over that rule. Now, you'll have to be punished."

Her eyes widened and her body began to hum. She should be scared or at least nervous but everything they'd done so far had been wonderful.

"I see that you think you're going to enjoy it." He leaned down until his mouth was next to hers. "But you're wrong. There won't be any enjoyment for you. Just frustration."

She touched his cheek, loving the roughness of his morning stubble. It'd felt better than good between her thighs. His eyes softened and he turned, kissing the palm of her hand.

"But first, I'm going to fuck you."

"Yes, Sir." She grinned. She could hardly wait.

He grabbed her legs and put them against his chest so they rested along his shoulders.

"Ah..." She was practically laying on the counter and it wasn't all that comfortable.

He grabbed a condom from his pocket, unzipped his pants and let them fall to the floor. His cock was hard and standing straight and she'd forgotten for one moment what an impressive thing it was. She still couldn't believe it actually fit inside her, but the hint of soreness between her legs was proof that he had indeed been there.

He tore open the condom and slid it down his cock. He grabbed himself, stroking as he stepped closer. "This is for me, Maggie. I didn't come, but you did. Without permission."

"Are you say..." Her breath hitched as the heat of his head rubbed against her pussy. All that passion she'd just released was tightening again.

"I'm saying..." He grabbed her wrists holding them over her head "That I'm going to fuck you like I want, not for your pleasure but mine."

He slid the tip inside and she gasped, watching as that long, thick cock disappeared inside of her. It seemed impossible, but it wasn't. She could feel him so deep in this position.

"Fuck, you feel good." He pulled almost all the way out and thrust back inside, fast and hard.

She groaned. She was still tender from last night but beneath that pain was pleasure, pure and raw.

"Tell me it feels good. Tell me, I don't have to stop or go slow." He pulled out again, waiting.

"Please."

"What? Please what?" There was a hint of panic in his voice.

"However, you want, Sir. It feels good."

That was all it took. He was back inside in one hard slide and then he was moving. Her body rocked with his thrusts, sparks of pleasure igniting as he filled her over and over. He let go of her hands to grasp her thighs, keeping her legs straight along his body. His thrusts grew faster and harder and even the tinge of soreness disappeared as passion and desire surged through her. She reached for him.

"Play with your tits." His face was tight and his voice gruff.

Her hands dropped to her sides. She'd never done that in front of anyone.

"Maggie..." There was a warning in his tone.

She was already going to be punished, unless this was her punishment. She smiled and his gaze darkened to almost black.

"Touch your breasts. Now."

She rested her palms on her nipples.

"Pinch them."

She did, sending pleasure shooting through her body to her pussy, making her clench around him.

"Fuck, yes. Do it again."

She did, again and again, clinging to his cock with every pinch. His movements were getting wilder. He was close but she wasn't there yet.

"Terry wait. I'm not...Sir, please."

"You disobeyed."

"Please." She'd cry if he finished and she didn't come.

He flattened his hand on her abdomen, pressing downward as he fucked her. Each thrust now caused his dick to hit a bundle of nerves deep inside her body. It was pleasure and pain, spiraling together. She clutched at the counter, no longer able to play with her breasts—the feelings were too good and coming too fast. She was going to come. "Terry...Sir...Yellow."

"Come, Maggie. Come for me." He bent a little, hitting that spot hard with his next thrust and the next, until she spiraled out of control.

She clung to his cock but he thrust again and again before his fingers dug into her hips as his head fell back and his dick jerked inside of her.

When she opened her eyes, he was still buried deep inside her body. His hands were on the mirror and he was watching her.

"You should finish your breakfast. You're going to need it today." He trailed a finger around her nipple and his dick started to come to life.

She sat up. "Oh, no." She shoved on his chest and he let

her push him away. She gasped a little as he pulled out of her, missing him already. She slid off the counter, tugging her bra and shirt down.

"Don't bother. I'm only going to strip you bare again."

"I can't." She pulled on her underwear and pants before kissing his cheek. "I'd love to, really, but I have to go." She stepped away. "I had fun last night, but I have to go home." Unfortunately, her fantasy was over. Reality had returned and she had a house to pack.

****

Thanks for reading the first part of The Dom's Submission series. I hope you enjoyed the story. Next is a peek at book 2 in The Dom's Submission Series and after that are sneak peeks at some other books in the La Petite Mort Club series.

PART TWO – HIS MISSION

Terry had found his perfect little sub and wasn't letting Maggie get away that easily. He wasn't tired of fucking her yet. "Why do you have to leave? Your kids don't come home until Sunday."

"I have to work tonight." Maggie looked in the mirror and straightened her hair.

"What time?"

"Five."

"That's hours from now." Which gave him hours to convince her to call off. It was a shitty job anyway.

"I have to pack." She headed into the bedroom.

"Pack?" He followed, watching the way her ass bounced as she walked. God, he wanted to slap that butt and watch it jiggle as he fucked her.

"Yeah, I have to move in a couple of weeks."

"Why?" She'd better not be moving far away. They were nowhere near done with their...It wasn't a relationship, but unlike with his other subs, he hadn't drawn up a contract. It didn't matter what they called it. They were not done with each other.

"Can't afford to stay there since the divorce."

"Where are you moving?"

"Not far." She walked faster into the living room.

That was good, but she was hiding something. As a lawyer, he was quite familiar with evasive answers. He leaned against the dining room table. "Where?"

"Down the street a bit." She looked around the living room. "Have you seen my purse?"

He pointed to the table next to the door.

She walked over and grabbed her phone from her purse.

"What are you doing?"

"Calling an Uber."

"Don't." They'd been over this, again and again. "You can use my car. It's just sitting in the garage."

"I'm not taking your car."

"Why? I don't use it. No one does." He'd never met such a stubborn woman. "I bought it for my daughter as a college graduation present but she wanted a European trip. So, the car sits there." He walked across the room toward her. "You'd be doing me a favor. It's not good for cars to sit. They need to be driven." Like women needed to be fucked. "Plus, you agreed to obey me."

"That's only when...you know." She blushed as she waved her hand. She was adorable.

"When we fuck. Say it." He stepped closer to her, letting her feel the pull of attraction between them.

"No. You know what I meant." She stepped aside and started to punch numbers into her phone.

He snatched it from her.

"Hey, give that back."

He couldn't believe he was reduced to this. He held it in the air out of her reach, as his mind scrambled for a way to make her stay.

"Stop acting like a child and give me my phone."

She was right, but she brought out the worst in him. "If you won't take the car, at least, let me drive you home." He handed her the phone.

She frowned but nodded. "Thank you."

"Give me a moment." He went into his bedroom and came back with his keys and his gym bag. Hopefully, he wouldn't need the change of clothes because of working out. "Ready?"

He opened the door to the garage and stepped aside so she could go first. She eyed the bag but kept her suspicions to herself like a good little sub.

You can save some money by buying the box set (click the link below)

Find out what happens next.
https://ellisoday.com/books/his-mission/

See below for a sneak peek of Interviewing for her Lover (Nick and Sarah's story) and The Voyeur (Patrick and Annie's story). They're both free on all ebook retailers. You can get the entire Six Nights of Sins series (Nick and Sarah's six nights of kinky fun) for free. A thank you gift for joining my newsletter.

Here's What You Get When You
Join My Readers' Group

Win Before You Can Buy
Exclusive Giveaways
Free Books
Sneak Peeks

Go to my website or email me for details:

https://www.EllisODay.com

authorellisoday@gmail.com

Interviewing For Her Lover

CHAPTER 1: SARAH

"Do I have to take off my clothes?" Sarah tugged on the hem of her black dress. It was shorter and lower cut in the front than she normally wore, but the Viewing was about finding a man for sex and according to Ethan men liked to look.

"No." Ethan turned her away from the door and forced

her to look at him. "You don't have to do anything you don't want to do."

She stared into his blue eyes. Why couldn't he be interested in her? She'd only met with him five or six times, but she trusted him. He ran his business, La Petite Mort Club, very professionally and he was gorgeous with his sandy brown hair, strong cheekbones and vibrant blue eyes. Sex between them would be good. Easy. He was attractive and…not for her. She didn't want decent sex or good sex, she wanted mind blowing, screaming orgasms and that wouldn't happen between him and her because there was no chemistry, no attraction.

"Listen to me." He moved his hands to her shoulders and gave her a gentle shake. "You aren't selling yourself to the highest bidder. You're looking for a partner. One who'll"—he grinned—"turn you on in ways you can't even imagine."

She glanced at the door where the men waited. Waited for her. Waited to decide if they wanted to fuck her. "I'm a bit nervous."

"About what?"

This was embarrassing but she'd been honest with him up to this point. She'd had to be. He was helping her…had helped her to choose the five men in the other room.

"What if none of them…"

"They will want you." He touched her chin, turning her face toward him. "A few of them may back out after this but not because they don't want you."

"Yeah, right."

"I'm only going to say this once. You're beautiful and different, unique."

"That's not necessarily a good thing." She had long legs and a nice body—trim and firm—but with her auburn hair and green eyes she was cute at best, not gorgeous. The men she'd chosen were all rich, good looking and powerful. They could have anyone they wanted.

"It's exactly what they want, or most of them anyway." He took her hand and led her closer to the door.

She leaned on his arm, hating these shoes. She should've stuck with her flats but Ethan had given her a list of what she should wear and high heels were on the top. She'd found the smallest heels in the store and by Ethan's look when he'd first seen her she might've been better off going barefoot. He'd met her at the private entrance and his gaze had been appreciating as it'd skimmed over her dress, until he got to her feet. Then he'd frowned and shook his head.

"Finding the right men for you wasn't easy." He

stopped at the door.

"Thanks a lot." She shifted away from him, his words hurting a little. She hadn't been sure of her appeal to the opposite sex in a long time, not since the early years with Adam.

"It's not because you aren't beautiful but because you want to be dominated and you want to dominate—"

"I do not want to dominate." All she could picture was a woman in black leather with a whip and that wasn't her, not at all.

"If you say so." He smiled a little. "But, you do want to lead the scene. Right? Because that's what—"

"Yes." Her face was red. She could feel it. She didn't want to talk about her fantasies again. It'd been embarrassing enough the first time, but he'd had to know what she wanted to compile a list of candidates.

"Most at the club are either doms or subs. Very few are switches." His eyes raked over her. "That's what's so special about you. You want it all and...that's what made choosing these men difficult."

He'd given her a selection of twenty-two men who might be interested in what she wanted. She'd narrowed it down to seven. Two had been uninterested when he'd approached. That'd left her with the five who'd see her in person for the first time tonight, but she wouldn't see them. That'd come after the Viewing when she interviewed any who were still interested.

"Remember what you want. This is your deal. You call the shots. At least a little." He kissed her forehead. "But don't refuse to give them anything. You don't want a submissive."

"No." That didn't turn her on at all and she only had eight weeks. One night each week for two months before she'd go back to her lonely life, her lonely bed, dreaming of Adam.

"You can do this." He pulled a flask from his jacket and unscrewed the lid. "For courage."

"Thanks." She took a large swallow, the brandy too thick and sweet for her taste but it was better than nothing.

"Now, go find your lover."

She laughed a little but sadness swept through her. There'd be no love between this man and herself. This would be sex, fucking. That's all. The only man she'd ever love, her only lover, was dead. This was purely physical. "Thank you again." She stood on tip-toe and kissed his cheek. He may be gorgeous and run a sex club but he was a good man, a good friend.

She turned and opened the door and walked into the

room, trying to stay balanced on these stupid heels. Men wouldn't find them so attractive if they had to wear them. The room was dark except for one light highlighting a small platform. That was for her. She stepped up onto the small stage. The room was silent but they were there, above her, hidden behind the one-way mirrors, watching and deciding if they wanted to take the next step—to eventually take her.

She stared into the blackness of the room. It wasn't huge but its emptiness made it seem vast. She glanced upward, the light making her squint and she quickly stared back into the darkness. This was arranged for them to see her. That was it. She'd get no glimpse of them yet. She'd seen their pictures, chosen them but meeting them in person would be different. A picture couldn't tell her their smell or the sound of their voices.

She tugged at her dress where it hugged her hips, wishing the questions would start, but there was only silence. She shifted, the heels already killing her feet. Ethan hadn't liked them and if they weren't going to impress, she might as well take them off. She moved to the back of the stage, leaned against the wall and removed her shoes. As she returned to the center of the stage a man spoke, his voice loud and commanding almost echoing throughout the room.

"Don't stop there. Take off your dress."

She bent, placing her shoes on the floor. That wasn't part of the deal. She wasn't going to undress in front of five men, only one. Only the one she chose. She straightened. "No."

"What?" He was surprised and not happy.

"I said no. That's not part of the Viewing."

"I want to see what I'm getting."

She stared up toward the windows, squinting a little. She couldn't tell from where the voice had come. The speaker system made it sound as if it were coming from God himself. "And you will if I pick you."

Another man laughed.

"It's not funny. She's disobedient," said the man with the loud voice.

"Not always. I can be obedient." These men liked to be in control but sometimes, so did she.

"Will you raise your dress? Just a little," asked another voice.

"Didn't you see enough in the photos?" She'd applied a few months ago for this one-time contract. She'd been excited and nervous when she'd received the acceptance email with an appointment for a photography session.

She'd never had her picture professionally taken, since she didn't count school portraits or the ones her parents had had done at JCPenny's. She'd been anxious and a little turned on imaging wearing her new lingerie in front of a strange man, so she'd been disappointed to find the photographer was an elderly woman, but the lady had put her at ease and the photos had turned out better than she'd expected. She glanced up at the mirrors, hoping she wasn't disappointing all the men. That'd be too embarrassing.

"Those were…nice, but I'd like to see the real thing before deciding if you're worth my time."

She raised a brow. "You can always leave." She shouldn't antagonize him. She was sure the bossy man had already decided against committing to this agreement. Disobedience didn't appeal to him. That left four. If she didn't pick any of them, she could go through the process again, but she didn't think she would.

The man chuckled slightly. "I know that, but I haven't decided I don't want to fuck you. Not yet, anyway."

The word, so harsh and vulgar excited her. It was the truth. That was what she, what they were all deciding. Who'd get to fuck her. It was what she wanted, what she'd agreed to do, and as much as she dreaded it, she wanted it. She was tired of being alone. She missed having a man inside her—his tongue and fingers and cock.

"Do any of you have any questions?" She clasped her dress at her waist and slowly gathered it upward, displaying more and more of her long legs. She ran. They were in shape. The men would like them.

"Lower your top," said the same man who'd told her to take off her dress.

She didn't like him. If he didn't back out, she'd have Ethan remove him from her list. He was too commanding. He'd never allow her to be in control.

"I don't know if he's done looking at my legs yet." She continued raising the dress until her black and green lace panties were almost exposed.

"Very nice and thank you," said the polite man.

"You're welcome." This man might work. She shifted the dress up another inch before dropping it, giving them a glance at her panties.

"Now, your top," said the bossy guy.

She lowered her spaghetti string off one shoulder, letting the dress dip, but not enough to show anything besides the side of her bra.

"More," he said.

"No." She raised the strap, covering herself. She didn't like this man and wished he'd leave. She'd kick him out but that wasn't part of the process and they were very firm about their rules at this club.

"He got to see your pussy. Why don't I get to see your tits?"

"You got to see as much as he did." She was ready to move on. She bent and picked up her shoes. "If there's nothing else, gentleman, we can set up times for the interview process."

"Turn around," said another man.

It was a command, but she didn't mind. There was a politeness to his order and something about the texture of his voice caused an ache between her thighs. There was a caress in his tone but with an edge and a promise of a good hard fuck.

"Are you going to obey?" His words were whisper soft and smooth.

"Yes." That was going to be part of this too. Her commanding and him commanding. She dropped her shoes and turned.

"Raise you dress again."

She looked over her shoulder at where she imagined he sat watching her.

"Please." There was humor in his tone.

She smiled and slowly gathered the dress upward. She

stopped right below the curve of her bottom.

"More. Please." There was a little less humor in his voice.

She wanted to show him her ass. She wanted to show that voice everything but not with the others around. This would be just her and one man, one stranger. That was one of her rules. "No. Only if you're picked do you get to see any more of me than you have." She dropped her dress, grabbed her shoes and walked off the stage and out the door.

She was going to have sex with a stranger. She was going to live out her fantasies for eight nights with a man she didn't know and would never really know, but she wasn't going to lose who she was. She'd keep her honor and her dignity which meant she had to pick a man who'd agree with her rules.

Get your free ebook copy.

http://books2read.com/u/3nYKo6

ELLIS O DAY

LA PETITE MORT CLUB
THE
VOYEUR
THE VOYEUR SERIES

The Voyeur

CHAPTER 1: ANNIE

Annie finished making the bed and gathered the sheets from the floor, keeping them as far away from her body as possible. These sex rooms were disgusting and Ethan was a jerk making her work as a maid. She almost had her Bachelor's Degree in Culinary Arts, but he'd refused to hire her for the kitchen—too many men in the

Ellis O. Day

kitchen. The only job he'd give her at La Petite Mort Club was as a maid and unfortunately, she needed the money too badly to refuse.

She stuffed the dirty sheets into the cart and hurried out the door. She had almost thirty minutes before she had to be at the next "sex room." She hid the cart in a closet and darted down a back hallway, staying clear of the cameras. Julie, the woman who supervised the daytime maids, was a real bitch. If she were caught sneaking away from her duties, she'd be assigned to the orgy rooms every day. Right now, they all took turns cleaning that nightmare. She swore they should get hazard pay to even go in those rooms.

She slipped through a doorway and hurried to the one-way mirror. She stared at the couple in the next room. From her first day here, she'd been curious about the activities at the club. She was twenty-four and wasn't a virgin but she'd never, ever done some of these things.

The woman in the room below was tied to a table, legs spread and wearing some sort of leather outfit that left her large breasts free and her crotch exposed. She had shaved her pussy and her pink lower lips were swollen and glistening from her excitement. The man strolled around the table as if he had all night. He still had his pants on but had removed his shirt. His arms and chest were well defined but he had a slight paunch. His erection tented his pants and Annie felt wetness pool between her legs. She had no idea why watching this turned her on but it did.

186

Ever since she'd accidentally barged in on that guy and girl in the Interview room, she couldn't stop watching.

The man below ran his hand up the woman's inner thigh, glancing over her pussy. The woman thrust her hips upward and Annie ran her own hand between her legs. The man's mouth moved but Annie couldn't hear anything and then he slapped the woman across the thigh hard enough to leave a red mark. Annie jumped. She wasn't into that, but she couldn't stop watching the woman's face. At first, it'd contorted in pain but then it'd morphed into pleasure. The man hit her again and then bent, kissing the red welts—running his tongue across them as his fingers squeezed her nipple.

Annie clutched her thighs together, searching for some relief. Her panties were soaked. It wouldn't take but a few strokes to make her come. She started to slide her hand into her pants.

"Having fun?" asked a deep voice from behind her.

She spun around, her heart dropping into her stomach. "Ah...I was just finishing cleaning in here." Damn, she should've closed the door but she hadn't expected anyone in this area. The rooms were off limits on this floor until tonight and she was the only one assigned to clean here.

He shut the door and locked it before strolling toward her. She'd seen him around the Club, but more than that she remembered him from the military photos her brother, Vic, had sent to her. She carried one of the three of them—Vic, Ethan and this guy, Patrick—in her purse. He'd been attractive in the picture, but now that he was older and in person he was gorgeous. He had dark green eyes, brown hair and a perfect body. He stopped so close to her his chest almost brushed against her breasts. She was pretty sure it would if she inhaled deeply. She really wanted to take that deep breath and feel his hard chest against her breasts.

"Don't let me stop you from enjoying the show."

"I...I wasn't. I should go." She started to walk past him but he grabbed her hand.

His grip was warm and strong but loose enough that she could pull free if she wanted. She didn't. Even though she only knew him from her brother's pictures and letters, she'd had many fantasies about him when she'd been in high school. Her gaze dropped to the front of his pants and her mouth almost watered. He was definitely interested. She dragged her eyes up his body, stopping on his face. He smiled at her.

"There's nothing to be embarrassed about. Watching turns us all on." He kissed the back of her hand and she jumped as his tongue darted out, tasting her skin.

"I...I should go." She didn't move.

"No, you should watch." He dropped her hand and grabbed her shoulders, gently turning her toward the mirror. He trailed his hands up and down her arms. "Watch."

The man in the other room was now sucking on the woman's breast as his fingers caressed her pussy.

"Would you like to hear them? Or do you like it quiet?" His voice was a rough whisper against her ear.

"Sound, please." She wanted to hear their gasps and moans. She wanted to close her eyes and pretend it was her. She shifted, squeezing her thighs together.

He chuckled as he moved away. She felt his absence to her bones. He'd been strong and warm behind her and for a moment she'd felt safe, safer than she had since her brother had come back from the war, broken and sad, and her father had started drinking again.

The woman's moans filled the room and Patrick came back to stand behind her, this time placing his hands on her waist.

"I'm Patrick," he said against her ear.

She couldn't take her eyes from the scene in front of her. The woman was almost coming as the man thrust his fingers inside of her.

"What's your name?" He nipped her neck and she jumped.

"I…I…" If she told him her name, he might say something to Ethan. Ethan would kill her if he knew she was in here watching.

"Tell me your name." His lips trailed along her neck and she tipped her head giving him better access.

The guy was kissing his way down the woman's body. Annie wanted to touch herself, to make herself come but Patrick was here.

He nibbled her ear. "Why won't you tell me your name?"

"I…I'll get in trouble." She rubbed her ass against his erection, hopefully giving him a hint.

"Tease." His hand drifted down her stomach, stopping right above where she wanted him to touch. "Tell me your name or I'll make you suffer." He unbuttoned her pants and left his hand—warm, rough but immobile—resting on her abdomen.

"I can't." She stood on tip-toe, hoping his hand would lower a little but he was too tall or she was too short. He had to be almost six foot and she was barely five-foot four. "I could get fired and I need this job."

"Darling, Ethan won't fire you for fucking a customer."

"We can't." She spun around. She hadn't thought this through. He was her fantasy come to life and she wanted him to be hers just for a moment, but Ethan would find out and then she'd be in deep shit.

"Don't worry. I'm a member and you work here, so we're both clean." He hesitated, his hands tightening on her hips. "Are you protected?"

"What?" She had no idea what he was talking about.

"Ethan makes sure everyone at the Club is clean but only the...some of his employees are required to be on birth control." He ran his hands up her sides, getting closer and closer to her breasts. "Are you on birth control?" His eyes darkened as they dropped to her tits. "If not, it's okay. There are other things we can do."

Oh, she wanted to do everything his eyes promised, but she couldn't. "No, I'll get in trouble. I need this job. I have to go." She tried to move but her feet refused to obey, so she just stared at his handsome face.

"Are you sure?" He bent so he was almost eye level with her. "I promise. Ethan won't care. A lot of maids become…change jobs. The pay's a lot better." His eyes roamed over her frame. "Especially, for someone as cute as you."

Ethan would kill her before letting her become one of his pleasure associates.

"I could talk to Ethan for you." His hands moved up her body, stopping right below her breasts.

Her nipples hardened and she forgot everything but what he was making her feel. He ran his thumb over one of them and she leaned closer, wanting him to do it again.

He did. He continued rubbing her nipple as he spoke. "I could persuade him to let me…handle your initiation into club life."

Her heart raced in her chest. It could be just her and him doing all these things she'd seen. Her pussy throbbed but she couldn't do it. She wouldn't do it. She couldn't have sex for money. Her parents were both dead but they'd never understand and she couldn't disappoint them. "No. I can't do that…not for money." Her eyes darted to the door. She needed to get out of there before she did something she'd regret.

"That's even better." He smiled as he stepped closer. "We can keep this between us. No money. Only a man and a woman." He leaned down and whispered in her ear, "Giving each other pleasure. A lot of pleasure. In ways you haven't even imagined."

There were moans from the other room and she glanced over her shoulder. The man's face was buried between the woman's thighs.

Patrick turned her around, pulling her against him and wrapping his arms around her waist. "Are you wet?"

"What? No." She struggled in his arms, her ass brushing against his erection again.

"Oh fuck. Do that again." He kissed her neck, open mouthed and hot.

She stopped trying to get away. She wanted this…this moment. She shouldn't but she did, so she wiggled her butt against him again. He was hard and long and her body ached for him. It'd been too long since she'd had sex. She needed this.

"Would you like me to touch you?" His hands drifted over her hips and down her thighs.

She'd like him to do all sorts of things to her. She nodded.

"Say it." His words were a command she couldn't disobey.

"Yes."

"Yes, what?" He untucked her shirt from her pants.

"Touch me. Please." She was already pushing her hips toward his hand. She wanted his hand on her, his fingers inside of her.

"Are you wet?" he asked again.

She inhaled sharply as he unzipped her pants.

"Don't lie to me. I'll find out in a minute."

She'd never talked dirty during sex and she wasn't sure she was ready to do that with a stranger. Her heart skipped a beat. Maybe, she shouldn't be doing any of this with a stranger. She grabbed his hand. "Maybe, we shouldn't."

The woman below cried out and the man straightened, wiping his face and unbuttoning his pants.

"Watch. The main event is about to happen." Patrick's hot breath tickled her neck.

Her gaze locked on the man's penis. It was large and demanding. He straddled the woman, grabbing his cock.

"Don't you want to feel some of what they feel?" He nibbled on her ear and then neck. "I can help you."

She may not know him, but she trusted him. He was a former marine. He'd been a good friend of Vic's. He wouldn't hurt her and she needed to come. She loosened her grip, letting go of his hand. He slipped inside her pants, caressing her pussy through her underwear. His fingers were long and strong. She closed her eyes, leaning against him as he stroked her.

"You're already so wet and hot." His breath was a warm caress on her ear. "But, I'm going to make you wetter and then, I'm going to make you come." His other hand shoved her pants down, giving him more room to work. "Open your eyes and watch the show."

She did as he said. The man was inside the woman, thrusting hard and fast. The woman was moaning and trying to move but the restraints kept her mostly helpless.

"Fuck, you're soaked." Patrick's hand cupped her and she arched into his touch, rubbing her ass against his erection. He shoved his hand inside her underwear, his finger running along her folds until he slipped one inside.

"Oh." She grabbed his hand—not to push him away, but to make sure he didn't leave.

He smiled against her hair. "Don't worry, baby. I won't stop." He stroked his finger inside of her and his wrist brushed against her clit.

She needed more. She needed to touch him, feel him. She turned her head, wrapping her arms up and around his neck. He kissed her. It was desperate and wild, but he stopped too soon.

"They're almost done. You don't want to miss it."

She turned back to the mirror. The man below continued to fuck the woman as Patrick finger-fucked her. His other hand slipped under her shirt to her breast. His lips sucked her neck as he rocked his erection against her ass. He was everywhere, and she was so close. The muscles in her legs constricted. Her hips tipped upward.

"Wait, baby," he groaned in her ear, as he pushed a second finger inside of her. "Just a few more minutes."

His fingers were stretching her and it felt wonderful. She moaned, long and low as he thrust harder and faster, almost matching the pace of the man in the other room. She could almost imagine it was Patrick's cock and not his fingers inside of her.

"Oh...oh," she cried out. He was pushing her toward the edge. Her body was spiraling with each pump of his fingers. She was going to come—right here while watching that couple. It was so dirty and so wrong and it only made her hotter.

The woman below screamed and her body stiffened. The man thrust again and again and then grunted his release.

"Show's over." Patrick nipped her neck at the same time he pressed down on her clit with his thumb, sending her shooting into her orgasm.

She trembled and he pulled her close, his hand still cupping her pussy and his fingers still inside of her. When her heartbeat had settled, he removed his hand and bent, pulling off her shoes and removing her pants before lifting her and carrying her to the wall.

"My turn." He wrapped her legs around his waist.

Her phone rang. "My work phone. I...I have to answer it."

"When we're done." He unzipped his pants.

"Annie, answer the phone. I know you're around here. I can hear it ringing you stupid bitch," yelled Julie.

"Oh, shit." She shoved Patrick away, and ran across the room, grabbing her clothes off the floor. "It's my boss. She'll kill me if she finds me like this."

"I'll take care of Julie." He headed for the door, zipping up his fly. "Don't move." He grinned over his shoulder at her. "You can take off your pants again, but other than that, don't move."

"No. Please." She raced over to him, grabbing his arm. "I need this job." And Ethan could not find out about this.

"She won't fire you. She can't. Only Ethan can fire you." He bent and kissed her.

His lips were gentle and coaxing this time and her body swayed into him. He pulled her even closer and she could feel his cock, thick and heavy, pushing against her. Her pussy tightened again in anticipation.

"Damnit, Annie. This is going to be so much worse if I have to call your stupid phone again. Get out here!" Julie was only a few doors down.

She grabbed Patrick and tugged on his hand. "Please, hide." She glanced around, looking for somewhere that would conceal a six-foot muscular man.

"I'm not going to hide from Julie."

Get your free ebook and find out what happens next.
http://books2read.com/u/38r9Ka

Coming soon:
GO TO MY WEBSITE TO SEE ALL MY BOOKS AND
TO SEE WHAT'S COMING NEXT
HTTPS://WWW.ELLISODAY.COM

ETHAN'S STORY
MATTIE'S STORY
A LA PETITE MORT CLUB CHRISTMAS
JAKE'S STORY
HUNTER'S STORY
DESIREE'S STORY

Email me with questions, concerns or to let
me know what you thought of the book. I
love hearing from readers.
authorellisoday@gmail.com

Follow me.
Facebook
**https://www.facebook.com/EllisODayRom
anceAuthor/**

Twitter
https://twitter.com/ellis_o_day

Ellis O. Day

Pinterest
www.pinterest.com\AuthorEllisODay

ABOUT THE AUTHOR

Ellis O. Day loves reading and writing about love and sex. She
believes that although the two don't have to go together, it's best
when they do (both in life and in fantasy).

Printed in Great Britain
by Amazon

20226428R00120